Enjoy
the marvel.

Richard
Jim Frost

The March to Kekionga

The March to Kekionga

Jim Pickett

First Edition – 2019

OAK CREEK
media
Bluffton, Indiana

Acknowledgements

I would like to recognize the following organizations and places who provided information, sources for information and have placed markers and monuments in significant historical sites that helped in making this project possible: Allen County-Fort Wayne Historical Society; Allen County Public Library, Fort Wayne, IN; Allen County Public Library Genealogy Department Center, Fort Wayne, IN; Andrew L. Tuttle Museum, Defiance, OH; Anthony Wayne Metroparks, Toledo, OH; Defiance Public Library, Defiance, OH; The Fallen Timbers Battlefield National Historic Site; Fort Miami National Historic Site; Fort Recovery State Museum; The Garst Museum, GreeneVille, OH; The History Center, Fort Wayne, IN; The Historical Society of Northwest Ohio; Indiana Daughters of the American Revolution; Kentucky Gateway Museum Center, Maysville, KY; Mary Penrose Wayne Chapter of the Daughters of the American Revolution; The Ohio Daughters of the American Revolution; The Ohio Historical Society and the Waterville Historical Society, Waterville, OH.

The following people provided maps, materials and information regarding the complex time period covered in the project: Alan Gaff, Leslie Hamman, Nancy Knapke, Mike Lake, Stan Pickett, Richard Rozevink and Dave Westrick.

Thank you to Melody Foreman for editing; Jacob Pickett for technical support; Ed Schwartz for publishing; Aaron Steele for producing the map of Wayne's March; and Amber Steffen for designing the book cover.

Thank you to my wife, Jane, for advice and support.

Finally, I would like to thank the law firm of **Weaner, Yoder, Hill and Weber, LTD.**, Defiance, Ohio, for giving me permission to use a painting by Professor Hermann Wiebe for the front cover.

Introduction

It is hard to imagine as travelers and citizenry view the open farmlands of Indiana and Ohio what it looked like less than two hundred plus years ago. For thousands of years, massive forests with some oak trees hundreds of years old dominated the landscape. Narrow trails initially made by animals and later tamped down by Native Americans weaved their way to key locations. The rivers were like the Interstate Highways of today.

Indian rivalries between Miami, Iroquois, Potawatomie and other tribes led to battles over territories. Eventually Europeans advancing from east to west; trapped, hunted, traded and intermarried with the Native Americans until wars over power and territorial rights came into play in a different dynamic.

In 1783, the United States with its independence victory over England, claimed the Northwest Territory that included today's States of Illinois, Indiana, Michigan, Ohio, Wisconsin and a part of Minnesota.

After the United States, under General Josiah Harmar, suffered an unexpected setback at the Miami towns in 1790 and Governor Arthur St. Clair, a major massacre defeat at the upper Wabash River in 1791, President Washington has to make bold decisions on how to subdue a Native American resistance. Hundreds of new American settlers have been either killed or captured traveling down the Ohio River or traversing trails westerly into investment speculator's U.S land. A Chief Little Turtle led Native American coalition and British antagonists are holding settlements back. Peace treaty attempts with an enemy that has defeated the United States twice appear fruitless. A Revolutionary War hero named Anthony Wayne has been selected to train a controversial standing army that cannot afford to be defeated. Washington gives Wayne awesome responsibilities to settle a region hundreds of miles from the Nation's Capital of Philadelphia.

Much takes place during a complicated time period between late 1791 and 1794. Washington's ultimate goal of a fort built at the Miami towns, or as the Indian's called it, Kekionga, 'the gathering place,' is being challenged.

The author utilizes over fifty sources to be as accurate as possible in a concise manner. Eighty five per cent of the names in this historical fiction adventure story were real people and although the writer takes some liberties, most of the events actually happened. Written as a sequel to *The Bones of Kekionga* or as a stand-alone novella, the author shares the Native American and the new American's side of the story through the 'voices' of the people who were there.

Prepare yourself to journey back in time to 1915 and then to 1791.

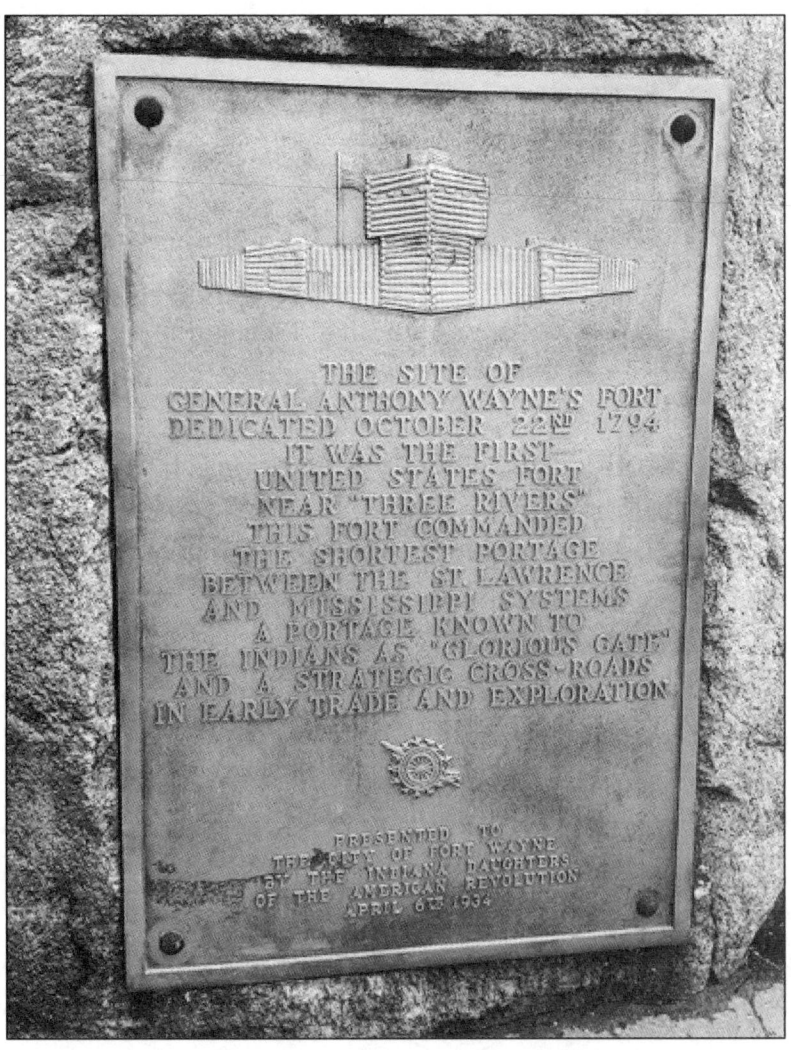

Michigan

Ft. Miami

Fallen Timbers

Ft. Deposit

St. Joseph River

Maumee River

Maumee River

Ft. Defiance

Great Black Swamp

Ft. Wayne

St. Mary's River

Auglaize River

Wabash River

Ft. Adams

Ft. Recovery

Anthony Wayne's March

Ft. Greenville

Ft. Jefferson

Ft. St. Clair

Indiana

Miami River

Ft. Hamilton

Ohio

N
W   E
S

Ft. Washington

Ohio River

Chapter 1

Late winter 1915 — East central district, Fort Wayne, Indiana

"Give her some gas, Nyle! Let's get up this hill and continue heading south on Clay Street!"

"Alright! Ha! We're up to ten miles per hour, Stan."

"Dad burn, that load of coal we're hauling is slowin' us."

"We're gonna make it, brother," says Nyle pushing the throttle.

"Good, good, this is Berry Street comin' up. Keep on goin'. Did you know General Wayne built that first American fort over there on the right?"

"You been talkin' to Bob Gavin again, haven't ya?" asks Nyle, attempting to accelerate the Mack AB three-speed pickup truck.

"Yeah, I like listening to his historical tidbits. Turn left here at Wayne Street."

"Gotcha."

"Geez, watch out for that trolley! You know they can't steer out of our way."

"Hey, I'm just getting use to this contraption. Do we go on Wayne as far as old Ben's lumber yard? Wonder if his sons, Harry and Elmer, are still his teamsters?"

"Nope. We're gonna turn before we get there. Keep going past Harmar Street, named after that General who was given a lickin' by Chief Little Turtle. Ya know, I bet he and his army traveled this street north into Kekionga."

"Aww, you and your history lessons. Ha. They didn't have streets back then."

"Turn left here at Begue Street."

"Umm, the Harrington's live in that two-story brick house on the right. Pull over here, Nyle. I'll go check if they're home."

After an initial greeting, Stan waves his former construction partner in, and the elderly Mrs. Harrington shows the two the basement door and tells them where the outside coal delivery window is located.

"Nice place you have, Ma'am," says Nyle attempting small talk. "How long you and Mr. Harrington lived here?"

"Oh, my poor departed husband passed away a couple months ago in the dead of winter. Oh, dear me! Sorry about that expression. I'm still getting used to him being gone. Rest his soul. Oh, I miss him."

"Sorry, Mrs. Harrington. Didn't mean to sadden ya."

"My husband always did the coal furnace chores. We have a laundry room up here so I never had to go down to that dirty old cellar. My nephew has been helping me, but he is out of town for a couple days, and this is the only day you fellas could come this week. Oh dear. Now you young men be careful going down the stairway."

"Don't worry, ma'am. Let me switch the light on. We'll figure things out down there," reassures Stan. "Uh-oh. No lights. May need a new light bulb. You got a lantern we can use, ma'am?"

"Oh dear, I think my husband kept one of those in the storage closet." The short, lean lady quick-steps her way to retrieve a kerosene burner lantern, a new bulb and a book of matches.

"Yes, here you go, boys. Now don't burn yourself."

"Thank you, ma'am. Here, brother, you take the lantern. I'll bring the bulb," offers Nyle. "Watch it, steps are kind of narrow."

"Yeah, I can see that," Stan remarks, advancing toward the bottom of the stairs. "Holy jeepers! Wait till you gaze on this, Nyle! You know what is down here, Mrs. Harrington?"

"Well now, you know my husband, his friends and our nephew are the only ones I know of who've gone down there!"

Nyle reaches the bottom of the stairs and is taken aback by the faint lantern light exposing a sight rarely seen.

"Dad burn! Skulls all the way around the basement wall's ledge. Must be fifteen of 'em!"

"This is the guy's house Mr. Gavin was tellin' us about a couple years ago," Stan responds.

"You're right. I remember him talkin' about this man, Harrington. I thought he was joking or it was just a rumor."

Screwing the light bulb in and looking up the stairs, Nyle calls to Mrs. Harrington. "You know you got skulls in your cellar?"

"Skunks? Skunks? Lordy, get them out of there—but don't get sprayed! It will stink the house up for a year!"

"No, no, skulls! Skulls! You know, skeletal skulls! You got skulls in your cellar!"

"Skulls?!" screams Mrs. Harrington.

Nyle, looking up the stairway, hollers, "Mrs. Harrington, now listen to me. You're gonna need to call the police and report this, okay?"

"Oh dear, I've never talked to the police in my life. Oh, I don't want to get in trouble."

"Don't worry ma'am. We've dealt with this before. You won't get in trouble," informs Stan.

Whispering to Nyle, he adds, "At least, I don't think she will."

"Well now, my historian brother. As I look closer, I see they've either been scraped, gashed or bashed. Signs of long ago warfare Mr. Gavin told us about."

"Oh dear, what am I going to tell the police? What has my husband and his friends been up to? Oh, I need to go down there and see them, but I'm afraid," rambles Mrs. Harrington.

"I don't know, Mrs. Harrington, but they look really old!" yells Nyle back up the stairs.

"Stan?" reflects Nyle smiling. "I'm beginning to acquire that historical curiosity you have. If these skulls could talk, I wonder what stories they'd have to tell?"

Chapter 2

"Giddup, Betsy! Heaah! Giddup, Pete!" yells E.J. Carlisle while snapping the bridle reins to get the supply wagon horses to pull faster.

"Better watch it, E.J. We'll have another breakdown and never will catch up with General St. Clair," says Bobby Fulton, E.J.'s good friend perched next to him.

Bobby, clutching his French Charleville musket, glances around and looks back at the two men escorting a train of fifteen packhorses, each loaded with beef rations, flour, salt and whiskey.

"Yeah, well," E.J. answers, "this trail isn't the smoothest road we've been on. No wonder we busted that wheel yesterday. Good thing Mr. Sutherland and Mr. McClellan in back of us stopped to help. I don't know how far ahead St. Clair is, but it still annoys me the army wouldn't halt to wait on us."

"There is nothing gonna hold up a 1600-man army and 200 camp followers short of an Indian ambush, E.J., let alone two sixteen-year-olds fixin' an old wagon wheel."

"Speaking of Indians, Bobby, seems a bit strange, but I haven't spotted one since we left Fort Jefferson yesterday morning."

"Come to think of it, you're right. Maybe St. Clair's army has scared them off," opines Bobby.

"That sounds like us a year ago," E.J. recalls, "braggin' about Harmar's army. We were lucky to get back to Fort Washington, according to that Shawnee Injun that Colonel Hardin captured. Why, if it wasn't for that night phenomenon Pastor was pointing out and Indian superstition, we'd of been in trouble."

"We were already in trouble, E.J.," reminds Bobby, hanging on while the wagon carrying muskets, clothing, tents, and blankets sways. "We lost your uncle and Ben in that battle at Kekionga."

E.J. snaps the reins while he thinks a bit.

"Unk was just startin' to get over the loss of his family to those Mingos back in Pennsylvania," recalls E.J. "Ben was a good friend, even though I hadn't known him that long. They were good fighters, too. Unk could really ride that cavalry stallion, swingin' that sword! Man, I miss those two. And Bobby, I want to thank you for saving my life and gettin' me back to camp."

"Don't mention it, E.J."

"Charlotte and her family have been real kind to us two," says E.J., thinking of his girlfriend.

"We've been through a lot," adds Bobby. "Hopefully, this General or Governor St. Clair -- whatever he calls himself -- learned from Harmar's mistakes. Building forts as we travel north is probably a good idea."

A couple of loud whistles are heard by the boys. Bobby turns around to see John Sutherland, a packhorse master, waving to stop.

"Hold up, E.J. Mr. Sutherland wants to speak with us."

As they wait on the supply train boss to walk up, the two companions clutch their muskets and gaze watchfully into the forest that lines each side of the trail.

"Fellas," informs Sutherland, "we've been traveling for four hours. Let's water these horses and take a break. To be honest, I thought St. Clair would have sent some cavalry back to see how we were doin' by now."

"Okay, Mr. Sutherland," obeys E.J. as he jumps down to fetch water into a bucket hanging from the bottom of the wagon.

"By the way, I heard you lads served with Harmar at Kekionga? I don't think you boys are even sixteen now, are ya? How'd you pull that off?"

"I know I am now," answers Bobby, smiling. "I don't know about E.J., but I signed up when the Penn militia was taking younger drummer boys, and I signed my name where they told me to. Why, I'd never seen a drum in my life until those kids started beatin' on 'em."

Sutherland just rolls his eyes. "What about you?" he says, glancing up at E.J.

"My uncle vouched for me, and I just signed. I think the recruiters for Harmar were having difficulty filling the ranks. Some other young ones got in too," claims E.J.

Approaching the three on the other side of the pack animals is part-time packhorse driver and part-time ranger Robert McClellan.

"Watch this, E.J. I saw McClellan do this yesterday," grins Bobby.

"Hey, Mac!" yells Bobby. "Show E.J. what you showed me yesterday."

Without breaking stride, the athletic McClellan leaps over a loaded-down horse and lands right in front of the astounded boys.

"Whoa," reacts E.J., "where'd you get those grasshopper legs?"

Mr. Sutherland just smiles and shakes his head.

"It's all raw God-given ability. Watch this," McClellan replies. He takes a three-step running start toward Pete and Betsy and bounds over both horses, landing on the other side and without breaking stride, grabs a bucket hanging under the wagon to fill with water.

"He reminds me of Fink who brought us down the Ohio," declares Bobby.

"They'd get along just fine making bets up and down that river," states E.J.

"Mike Fink, you say?" asks McClellan as he begins to water the packhorses. "Oh, I know that scalawag from our ranger days patrolling the Ohio. He's a real wild one, and yep, we won a few wagers. Ha!"

"Mac, what's it like being a ranger?" hollers Bobby up front, tending Pete and Betsy.

"Let's put it this way, I never met an Indian I liked. Although, I suppose, there might be a decent one or two. But I can tell ya some stories tha--"

E.J. suddenly jerks his head up the trail. "Shhh, you hear something? Sounds like, I don't know. I've heard that sound before. That's yelling or howling."

"Yeah, I hear it," offers Sutherland, "and it's gettin' louder."

Rushing down the roadway and through the forest on both sides are men, some in military uniform, others dressed as militia.

"Grab your guns, boys. Something is a happenin'," commands Sutherland.

Panic-stricken with blood flowing from their heads, arms and legs, warnings are shouted, "Turn around! Turn your horses and wagon around! Get out of here! It's a massacre! Injuns everywhere, and they're heading this way!"

Dozens of more terrorized soldiers stream by as Bobby, climbing aboard the wagon, grabs the reins trying to figure out how to turn the horse-drawn wagon in the opposite direction.

"Come on E.J., get up here!" yells Bobby.

"I can't! Charlotte and her family are up ahead with St. Clair!"

"Not anymore!" informs Sutherland, grabbing the bridles. "There goes the Governor on his horse right there! Let's go, kid! Let's get outta here."

Looking straight ahead, E.J. clutches his musket and advances through the seemingly endless evacuees. Alternating running and jogging, he startles the oncoming frightened troops focused on what's behind them.

A hundred yards up the trail, familiar co-teamster Benjamin Van Cleave is seen racing toward him.

"Better not go any farther, E.J.," says the breathless Van Cleave. "It's not good where you're heading. The army has been chased and ravaged by savages for forty-five minutes, and there aren't many alive behind me."

"I gotta find Charlotte," responds the fix-eyed E.J. staring ahead and moving forward.

Fifty yards farther, he sees a blond-haired girl running toward him holding the hand of and pulling along a six-year-old boy with two Delaware Indians pursuing and closing in. E.J., recognizing the situation, jumps away from a large oak tree to get a clean shot. His Charleville musket cracks a split second after he pulls the trigger. Gunpowder smoke blocks his vision briefly as he advances and observes an Indian falling dead just as the other warrior grabs the girl.

E.J. draws his pistol out as he reaches the flailing pair. Making contact with the Indian but unable to shoot, he accidentally drops the gun and finds himself on his back with the brave, having tossed Charlotte aside, approaching to jam a knife into his chest.

Bam!

The war-painted warrior grimaces and collapses on E.J.

Peering up, he sees Charlotte with her two hands on the pistol, still pointed at the Delaware.

"Charlotte, I thought that was you. You alright?" asks E.J., crawling out from under the dead Indian.

Seemingly in shock, Charlotte cannot answer and instinctively grabs her brother Phillip's hand. Releasing the pistol, she resumes moving south, not totally aware of what had just happened.

E.J. picks up the pistol and begins reloading while glancing back up the trail for any more warriors and then follows Charlotte.

A day later in the late afternoon at Fort Jefferson, twenty-eight miles south of St. Clair's massacre, survivors walk into the camp set up just outside the fort. Soldiers escort the injured through the gates to the surgeons while watchful eyes in the blockhouse above scan the outlying woods.

Bobby, Sutherland and McClellan are greeted by a disgruntled and chatty Captain Trueman. "I tell ya, I saw William Wells and Simon Girty with the Indians doing some awful things," exclaims Trueman, directing people with an arm in a sling. "I've seen 'em before, can't remember where, but that Wells with that red hair trying to look like an Indian. Why, he's a dirty dog."

"Over here, folks. Water and something to eat is near the fire," offers Private John Smith, a survivor at Kekionga and now of St. Clair's fiasco a year later.

"Is that you, Fulton?" Smith asks an exhausted Bobby.

"Smitty, I need a horse. I need a horse that's fresh. E.J. is back up the road looking for Charlotte and her kin."

"Nobody's goin' back out. Got orders, Fulton. If you haven't already, reload your gun, grab a bite and be ready to defend."

"I gotta find E.J."

"Bobby, I saw hundreds of Miami, Shawnee, Delaware, Potawatomie, Ottawa -- you name 'em -- in that attack. My best guess is they're movin' this way. So dang it, I ain't joking, don't be a fool."

Inside the Fort Jefferson headquarters lies Governor St. Clair suffering from gout and unable to stand.

"Alright, bring me a whiskey, Denny," orders St. Clair, trying to conduct a meeting. "I knew the Indians were out there, but dad burn it, I didn't think a major attack was imminent. I thought maybe some horse thieving or something."

"Governor, that whiskey won't help your gout," warns a tending army surgeon.

"Right now, I don't give a rat's crap, doctor. I had two dad-burned horses shot from under me and several musket balls sail through my hat during that battle and retreat. You think I care?

"Now, where was I? Lieutenant Denny?"

"Right here, sir."

"How many did we lose?"

"Maybe a thousand. I count about 300 returning to Fort Jefferson unhurt and 300 injured, Governor. We'll get a better number later today or tomorrow. We're still trying to make sense of it. Soldiers and citizenry are still coming in."

"Captain Slough, you in here?" the governor asks, lifting his head up slightly and peering around the room.

"Yes, Governor. I'm here."

"Why didn't you warn me? You were in charge of the scouting. Where the heck were you?"

"You were in bad shape, Governor, sick and everything. So I let second in command General Butler know of the circumstances. He was supposed to send that information to you, sir. I don't know what happened. Word is, he did not survive the attack, Governor."

"Last thing Washington said to me back in Philadelphia," divulges St. Clair, "was don't let the Indians surprise you. Dad burn if we didn't mess that up!"

"Sorry to interrupt you, Governor. We have a food and medical shortage here at Fort Jefferson," asserts Lieutenant Ebenezer Denny. "We need to head for Fort Washington as soon as possible. Can you do it, Governor? Can you ride a horse?"

"Captain Slough, get what's left of your spies out there patrolling," responds St. Clair. "It's a three-day march to Fort Washington. To allow for stragglers to come in, we'll leave the day after tomorrow if it's safe. The wounded will stay here under Captain Shaylor."

Meanwhile, outside Fort Jefferson, family and friends sporadically return.

"E.J.? E.J.!" calls Bobby as he sprints fifty yards from the camp to grab the reins of a large, black mare that Charlotte, Phillip and E.J. share a ride on.

"You three alright? Where's the rest of your family, Charlotte?" E.J. gently shakes his head as Charlotte stares straight ahead.

A few days later, the St. Clair's massacre survivors return to Cincinnati without incident.

Outside the door of Fort Washington's headquarters, Lieutenant Denny laments the massacre to close confidant General Josiah Harmar. "You were right, General. This army of St. Clair's was doomed the moment it left. Not trained up. Too many militia volunteers, not enough scouts."

"Started out too late in the year, as well," inserts Harmar. "Same mistakes I made. Denny, I'm sorry I talked you into going on this disaster."

"I understood your reasoning, General."

"Let's go in and get this out of the way, Lieutenant."

Harmar and Denny enter as St. Clair, feeling better physically, paces and listens to Adjutant General Winthrop Sargent's report.

"Of the 1,669 armed men we took, we lost 64 officers and 807 enlisted men killed or wounded. Throw in the packhorse drivers, blacksmiths, artificers, women and children, well, the count is over a thousand, sir," concludes Sargent.

"Tell us about the cannon and weapons lost, Captain Buell?" asks St. Clair.

"Lieutenant Denny, I hope you are taking notes. You're leaving tomorrow for Philadelphia to break the news to Washington."

Outside the Fort Washington walls, a survivors' camp is set up as the army pastor, comforting residents, walks up to E.J., Bobby, Charlotte and Phillip.

"Glad to see you got through that disaster," he says to the group. "Talk to me, tell me what happened?"

"I got a little taste of it, but Bobby and I weren't in the battle, Pastor. Charlotte and Phillip were there, though, and, well ..." stammers E.J.

"We were surrounded, Pastor, by Indians everywhere," opens up Charlotte for the first time. "At first, I heard a lot of shots and the militia, camped across the river, came running toward mom and I camped near the regulars. Many of these volunteers were yelling and had blood on them.

"Musket shots were going off everywhere. The Indians moved in closer. Women and children were praying, crying, weeping, sobbing. Some women grabbed the muskets of dead and wounded soldiers and fired. But the Indians came squeezing in all around us. We were surrounded. What were left of the men finally told what was left of the women to follow them and to head home. They made a bayonet charge through the Indians. My mother grabbed my one brother and I grabbed Phillip, and we followed father. He soon got into a bayonet fight protecting us but we kept running, and then my mother and one brother got knocked down and she yelled to keep going. Oh Pastor, it was awful," finishes a sobbing Charlotte, hugging her little brother.

Chapter 3

1791 – 1792 — Old Northwest Territory (Present-day Indiana and Ohio)

Thirty seven canoes, each with two or three Native Americans paddling hard, have a mile to go! The race to be the first to arrive at Kekionga is on. Digging deep into the St. Marys River water, Running Deer and his canoe mate nose ahead of the ten contending birch bark boat participants. Ignoring the waving and cheering squaws, children and old men along both sides of the riverbanks, Running Deer has an ulterior motive to finish fast. He is anxious to be reacquainted with Morning Bird.

The wigwams and cabins, large and small, that the Indians paddle past are blurs to the contestants as the canoes, loaded with captured booty from victory, navigate the last sharp bend in the river before arriving at the Kekionga landing area. Acquiring the few trinkets each warrior bet before the race is so exhilarating that Running Deer, upon slamming onto the beach, runs out of the canoe with his co-paddler, turns toward the late arriving racers, and raises his arms and screams, "Ayyyyayya!!"

That night, drums are pounding and chants are sung by hundreds of rollicking, victorious Native Americans celebrating the triumph over St. Clair's army a month earlier. Celebratory echoes are heard by French and British trappers and traders up and down the headwaters of the Miami of the Lake River, also known as the Maumee.

"Kekionga is getting back to normal, Henry," converses longtime resident Antoine Lasselle.

"Yes," British trader Henry Hay acknowledges in broken French, "I actually saw a lacrosse game being played on this warm winter day. I can't get over how they enjoy the racing and contests."

"On the other hand, what a mess Harmar's army left," complains Lasselle, "even after their defeat and being chased out of Kekionga a

-13-

year ago. But the replant of corn and gardens has gone well. Not sure where you were, but starvation was a real issue around here for a while, Henry. Thankfully, other villages took in many of the Miami, Delaware and Shawnee."

"This being a major trade passage," tells Hay, "I had to return here."

"Henry, from what I have heard from warriors, the conquest over some general named St. Clair was so devastating, they don't think the Americans will ever be back to the Ohio Territory."

"Yes, I have heard that confidence expressed also. It will be great that the natives and British can share this land together," says Hay smiling.

"Ahhhh! Ahhhhh!" is heard as another captive from the battle on the upper Wabash begins a long, tortuous death burning at the stake.

"AHHHH!" is heard as hundreds of Indians mock the cry of the victim.

Hay winces in response to the yelling from across the St. Joseph River and continues the conversation. "I never get used to the treatment of the enemy. Sometimes I think it may happen to me."

"Life in the wilderness, Henry? Nothing is for certain."

"Anyway, Lasselle, as I was going to say, my friend Alexander McKee and Simon Girty will be here after a visit to Fort Detroit to inform Lord Dorchester and some man named Simcoe what happened against St. Clair."

"Your empire should be more than willing to send redcoats and artillery in if the Americans want to invade again, don't you think? Even build a fort?"

"Well, only time will tell on that, but I agree. Listen, it's getting cold out here," comments Hay. "What do you say, Antoine? Let's go in my cabin, stoke the fire, have us some rum and celebrate the Indian victory ourselves."

Lasselle glances around before he ducks to enter the doorway and questions, "I wonder if our buddy Chief LeGris is around. He'd like this."

Young Miami warrior Running Deer glances at Morning Bird and can tell she is bothered by the celebration. As another tomahawk is driven into a pole, signaling the dancing warrior is ready to speak of his heroics, all the dancers sit down to listen.

Morning Bird gets up to move away from the circle of tribesmen and women. Running Deer, with blood-stained American scalps that he took from victims at St. Clair's defeat hanging from his belt, follows her. "Here is a blanket," offers Running Deer to Morning Bird. "It is cold away from the fire. Besides, it is from the victory over the invading whites."

"I will take it because it is from you and it will keep me warm, but I don't like it, Running Deer."

"St. Clair had many supplies we can use. It makes up for what Harmar did to us," reasons Running Deer.

As the two walk north along the St. Joseph River, the conversation in their native Algonquin continues.

"Not everyone wants war, Running Deer. I've said it before. There are tribes who feel they can live among the whites. I've helped heal some of the prisoners from their war injuries and have gotten to know them, only to watch them die at the stake or running the gauntlet."

"The Americans want our land, Morning Bird. We were here first," explains Running Deer, "and we will defend it with the help of the Great Manitou."

"I thought the Mound Builders were here first," questions Morning Bird. "Or was it the Iroquois that drove us out, and then we drove them out in war?" shaking her head in confusion. "When do the battles and wars end?"

"Both of those accounts appear to be true," admits Running Deer. "From the teaching of my grandfather and elders, the Great Spirit created man, animals and everything, and placed them somewhere that I am not sure. That was followed many moons later by a great flood that left only a few alive. The survivors re-multiplied the earth. I don't know the answer to the second question. All I know is that our people are here now, and we fight to survive and preserve our way of life."

"Don't get me wrong, Running Deer," responds Morning Bird, "I think it is wonderful that the tribes we were once enemies with are now united with us against the Americans. But what happens after we defeat the long knives?"

There are some from the northern country I do not like. I haven't told you this before, but some of their warriors, while passing through to join you in the Ohio land, made advances on us women. It was not pleasant."

"What? Which ones, Morning Bird?"

They are not here now. They are either at the Grand Glaize or have gone home. One individual I remember as being a very large Chippewa."

A few weeks later, British Indian agents McKee and Girty navigate their piroque, along with Blue Jacket of the Shawnees and Buckongahelas of the Delaware, to the shore on the St. Joseph side of Kekionga. Flooding forces the landing spot farther up the St. Joseph than normal. Many of the corn fields around the Miami towns are under water.

"Greetings, Little Turtle," speaks McKee, struggling with the Algonquin language. "There was tough paddling against the current coming from the Glaize."

"We brought some blankets and furs to trade," says Girty, trying to break the awkward silence of Little Turtle.

"If you want to trade, our friends Lasselle and Hay are up the St. Joseph River on the west side. They will be happy to accommodate you. But if you have brought food, that will be better. As you can see, the rains are delaying Kekionga's full recovery.

"Maybe it is time to move to the Glaize area, Little Turtle," suggests Buckongahelas. There is no serious flooding there, and we would be closer to the British."

"Kekionga has always been the meeting place and capital of Miami world. Many times over the years, our forefathers met here before going to battle. Most recently, the confederation met here before going to defeat St. Clair. Did we not cut our hair and paint our face in this very spot before departing for the upper Wabash?"

"It will only be temporary again, Little Turtle," speaks Blue Jacket.

"I do not like this impromptu meeting," glares Little Turtle. "Are the rumors of another American army true?"

"Ah, rumors are spoken everywhere, Little Turtle," answers Blue Jacket. "But if it is true, only death will await them."

Shifting his eyes to McKee, Little Turtle continues, "How can we be sure of the British? All they offer are rewards for American scalps."

"Oh, be assured, great war leader of the confederation, my friends and true countrymen, the British, see how you have taken the initiative and will join you if there is more warfare," answers McKee.

In west-central Ohio, peace attempts are made.

"Who do you say you are?" asks Chief Black Hoof. "A Colonel John Hardin? What are you doing so far north into Ohio Territory?"
Waiting for the interpreter, Black Hoof shades his eyes from the late-spring setting sun and looks over the American with a name that he knows well.

Hardin nervously stares back at Black Hoof, with good reason. With only an interpreter and guide as his escort, peace at this village does not look good.

"I bring a letter from the great White Chief called President George Washington," says Hardin. "I come from a place called Fort Washington on the Ohio River."

"I know of this Washington and of this fort you come from," says a frowning Black Hoof.

"Chief, it is a letter of concord offerings directly from the American president and a desire for my country's peace delegates to meet with you and all tribes at the Roche de Bout at the rapids on the Miami of the Lake, whenever a time can be established to discuss the discord between our peoples."

Not waiting for the interpreter to finish, "You, of all people," reveals Black Hoof, "wish to offer peace after the butchering raids you have made from Kentucky? You act as an equal and want peace after being with General Harmar at your defeat at Kekionga? What about St. Clair's massacre? Are you a fool, Colonel Hardin?"

"Look, I have gifts from President Washington as a good will intention," offers Hardin, knowing he is in trouble with a historically knowledgeable Black Hoof. "Besides that, Major Alexander Trueman is carrying a similar letter along the Maumee River toward the meeting place at the Roche de Bout."

"Look, it is late. We will take your gifts and consider your peace gestures. You camp here tonight and move on tomorrow," finishes Black Hoof turning away shaking his head.

A few weeks later, it is midsummer at Kekionga as a shaken Little Turtle looks into the eyes of his son-in-law, William Wells, and speaks. "What are you saying, Black Snake? Or are you Carrot Top? Or are you now the white American you have been denying these past few years?" "Father-in-law, another army is preparing to come to the land we call home. The Americans are relentless. They will keep coming," retorts Wells, now dressed in an American uniform taken from a victim at St. Clair's massacre.

"What you wear describes you perfectly, a traitor to your Miami brethren," declares Little Turtle. "I don't know who you are, Black Snake. You are torn between two worlds, one you have not known since you were a boy and one you know now."

"Many Miami and Shawnee wear these clothes, Little Turtle, as trophies of the great victory. After seeing the many whites massacred, my heart has changed. This constant warfare is no way to live. If it is not the Americans, it is the Iroquois or the Potawatomie or whomever the Miami look at cross-eyed."

"How do you switch after being adopted by a Miami mother and being raised in the Indian ways? How do you turn on us after killing so many of the whites you said you hated? What about your wife, my daughter, Sweet Breeze? What do you say to her and my grandchild?"

Wells continues in his fluent Algonquin language and adds sign language to emphasize his points.

"Little Turtle, what if you had to make a choice between your father's blood, a Miami, and your mother's blood of Mohican? What would you do?"

"You make a good point, son-in-law."

"I have already told Sweet Breeze and my Miami mother of my decision. Little Turtle, we must work together for peace between the two worlds. Do you not sense the British are using the Indians to fight their war?"

"Time will tell, but I want to believe the redcoats will come help the confederation."

"The ones I have met lack trust," expresses Wells.

"The Americans are extending themselves too far with their armies. Our spies tell of desertions and supply shortages," contends Little Turtle.

Staring at each other, the pause finally ends.

"Black Snake, you and Sweet Breeze will be welcomed in my home wherever that is. But I cannot guarantee your safety around my people," states the Miami Chief.

"If we meet in battle, Little Turtle, I promise not to harm you. Can you promise the same to me?"

Chapter 4

1792 – 1793 — Western Ohio Country, Philadelphia and the Ohio River

"Look out, Ben! Ben! Look out, Ben!"

"E.J., E.J., wake up," says Bobby, rolling over from his prone position nearby under a supply wagon. "You'll wake the whole camp, let alone the Indians."

Abruptly sitting up, E.J. bumps his head on the undercarriage of the wagon. In a sweat, he rubs his head, looking around.

"You're having a dream, E.J. You're okay," consoles Bobby.

Finally determining where he is, E.J. stares at his friend. "That was pretty real, Bobby, and they're happening more often. They make me not want to go to sleep at night."

"I've noticed," confirms Bobby. "I don't blame you."

"That Injun raid a couple days ago near Fort Hamilton didn't help. When we get to Fort Washington with this supply train, we have to refigure if this kinda life is worth it. Colonel Wilkinson defends us with a twenty-man escort, but if them Injuns get any kind of major force, we're done for."

"What are we goin' to do, E.J.?" reacts Bobby with his eyes closed. "We have to earn some money and keep savin'. Farmland isn't cheap, and this pays about as good as it gets."

"A dollar a day isn't much if you're going to lose your scalp. Indians are getting bolder, and the attacks are becoming more frequent according to some men."

"Geez, E.J., we've only been a part of one attack, and those Indians only made off with a couple packhorses," counters Bobby, rolling back over on one arm. "And what about Scott Traverse? Why, you heard him braggin' about taking supply trains all by himself to Fort St. Clair and beyond that to Fort Jefferson and never bein' bothered."

"All I know, Bobby, is that Charlotte lives in that fort in Cincinnati with Phillip and is afraid to come out for fear of Indians. It's nice the government allows her to stay in there since she lost her mom, dad and brother at St. Clair's defeat, but that's no way to live."

"Yeah, I know, she is fear-struck. But stragglers keep returning from that battle. Why, one kid had been gone from an Indian attack on his family in Kentucky three years ago. He lived with the Indians until he escaped and made his way back."

"Charlotte is holding out hope her parents will show up, but I don't know, Bobby." E.J. continues, "But I do know this, and hold on to your hat, Bobby. Charlotte and I are talking about getting married."

"Don't surprise me much," grins Bobby.

"Didn't think it would," smiles E.J. "I've always taken a shining to her, ever since I met her. We really like each other and all. But raising family around Cincinnati is dangerous, and I don't think that new army is coming anyway. It's just hearsay."

"They're not going to keep building forts like Fort St. Clair and supplying the other three for nothing."

"If the next army is anything like the last two, forget it. It's gonna be more of the same. In fact, it might be our scalps next," concludes E.J., lying back down.

At the capitol building in Philadelphia, peace on the frontier is desired.

"Secretary Knox, have you heard from the envoys of Captain Trueman or Colonel Hardin yet?"

"No, Mr. President, but I'm sure a message will arrive any day now. I have Lieutenant Denny up on Lake Erie talking to the Seneca and lake Indians to keep them away from the British and their Indian agents, the dirty scoundrels."

"General Putnam has been ordered to pursue a peaceful resolution at almost any price, correct?"

"Yes sir, Rufus is sending anybody with some influence or with your signed letter with them. If the signature of George Washington doesn't create peace, Mr. President, I don't know what will."

"Knox, you know as well as I do that it may come down to force, and the public here in Philadelphia or any of the fifteen states will not put up with another defeat like St. Clair's. For your sake and mine, Anthony Wayne better be the right man if peace isn't achieved through negotiations."

"He might be if we can keep him away from his favorite beverages."

"Dad burnit, Knox, all these generals drink. That's not an issue at this stage. We lost over sixty officers at St. Clair's slaughter, and Wayne is supposed to put together a 3000-man army."

"I know, I know, that's a pretty tall order," comments Knox.

"The man's had some failures lately as a politician and farming in Georgia, but I think he's hungry for what he is good at. He's smart, a strict disciplinarian, can diagnose a battle on the fly, and he's a fighter."

"You know him better than I do, sir. An interview or two can only go so far. You've seen him in action."

"Did I tell you about Wayne during the war, leading his men in a night surprise attack on the Hudson River at Stony Point? His men captured 450 British without firing a shot. Bayonets only! Killed 133 redcoats, nabbed fifteen cannons and lost only 100 men. Bayonets only, I tell you! He didn't want to alert the Brits of his attack. He's mad, I tell you! It was brilliant."

"We all had our successful moments in the war. We'll see, if we have to, what he can do this time around. Indian warfare, as you know Mr. President, is different. It terrorizes people.

"Recruiting is going slow, sir," Knox continues. "The last two defeats do not help. Wayne demands no militia. He wants fresh recruits to train up himself. He's busy doing that at Fort Pitt, although a new fort had to be built next to it. So if you hear of a Fort Fayette, it's the same place."

"Knox, I give Wayne full control of this war out west. Give him what he wants if you can get the allocations by Congress. Ha!"

"Yes sir, the contractors are lined up to meet his requests and will answer to me."

"This debacle in Congress about a standing army being dangerous to the citizens in this country is nonsense. Modern countries need a standing army," theorizes Washington, pacing the floor. "If it wasn't for France and Spain helping to train and fight with the militia we had, we would have been in trouble. According to witnesses and officers involved with Harmar and St. Clair, the forces the generals trained far outperformed the militia. We just didn't have enough of them."

"Wayne is issuing Von Steuben's Drill Blue Book to each officer. He will have the time to do it right, Mr. Washington. Running from the battle in cowardice will not be tolerated."

"Secretary Knox, if Wayne has to fight, he has been given the directive for his army to never be caught off guard by the enemy and to eventually build a fort and maintain it at the Miami towns, where the Miami of the Lake begins!"

Meanwhile, in a Fort Washington office, a secret meeting takes place.

"So you are William Wells, you say?"

"Come on, General Putnam, this is my brother. I'll witness for him. He was captured and taken into the Wabash and Eel River Indian territory when he was a kid. Doesn't the legend of his red hair give him away? He's been gone about nine years now."

"Sam, let him talk for himself. I'd a thought the redskins would have taken that red hair of yours and gotten double reward from the British by now," comments Rufus Putnam with a smirk. "You better be careful around this fort, Wells. Some survivors of St. Clair saw you in battle killing white folks. You have a reason why I shouldn't have you hung from a blockhouse by the neck till you are dead?"

"Rufus, dad burnit, he wouldn't have walked in the fort gates like a fool if he hadn't changed his ways," Sam Wells interjects.

"Sam, maybe you want to be hanging next to him?"

Putnam turns to a close friend and asks, "What do you think, Mr. Heckewelder? You've been surveying with me up and down the Ohio for many years and have seen some horrendous Indian deeds. Do we string these two up?"

"Let's hear what he has to say."

"Thank you," begins an anxious William Wells. Using the Algonquin language, Wells rattles off Miami, Shawnee, Delaware and Chippewa phrases that desire peace.

Putnam knows some of the utterances from his experience in the Ohio lands.

"I'm impressed, but anyone can memorize a few Indian words," reasons Putnam. "John, go get some redskin captives and bring them here."

"Yeah, I can do that, Rufus."

"We'll see if he can pass that test. If so, Mr. Wells, will you be willing to take a trip to the Grand Glaize and the rapids at the Maumee River, Roche de Bout, on behalf of the United States government?"

Outside the Fort Washington gates, goodbyes are said.

"Pastor, we've already made up our minds. Charlotte and I want to thank you for marrying us a few weeks ago, but we've made arrangements with a Colonel Pflueger, his wife Pluggy and Nine Eyes to help take his keelboat with our belongings back to our families in Pennsylvania."

"No offense, E.J., but you don't know much about these people," argues the pastor, "and it's dangerous on that river."

"It's dangerous here, Pastor," asserts Bobby. "We've given the life at Fort Washington and taking wagon and packhorse supplies through Indian territory long enough."

"Correction, Bobby, American territory," interjects the pastor. "Our country fought and died for it."

"Well, yeah, but we've been out west for almost four years now," interjects E.J., "and Charlotte and I keep having nightmares. We've both lost loved ones. Bobby and I almost got killed in that Fort St. Clair attack last fall, and that was with Major Adair and his Kentucky militia escorting us."

"Yes, I know way too much about death. I'm still consoling Colonel Hardin's widow. John told her he would be alright on his peace journey north with that letter from President Washington. Both his and Captain Trueman's bodies have been found mutilated."

"I'm sorry to hear that, Pastor. Add to that the attacks around here on settlers and packhorse loner Scott Traverse's scalping ... well, it's time to head back to Pennsylvania," bemoans Bobby.

Charlotte and Phillip walk out the fort gates for the first time in weeks, and Charlotte takes hold of E.J.'s hand. The pastor, in his long black coat and wide brimmed hat, escorts the four down to the waiting keelboat captained by Pflueger, and little is said until they near the Ohio River waterside.

"Another army is coming, folks," the pastor offers with a final parting comment.

Charlotte turns to the pastor, "The armies I've seen are no match for these savages, Pastor."

Near the keelboat walk plank, a voice from atop the vessel pierces another awkward silence. "Come on, folks, come on, get your luggage on here and down below," orders Pflueger with his hired hand, Nine Eyes, standing next to him watching several other men and a few women get aboard.

"You take care of my friends, okay Captain?" asks the pastor.

"It's Colonel, and sure enough, Father or Preacher or whoever you are," smirks Pflueger.

"Godspeed, kids," speaks a waving Pastor.

E.J. and Bobby nod and give a slight smile while helping Charlotte and Phillip get settled in the galley.

"Grab those poles!" hollers Nine Eyes. "Daylight's a wastin'. Hope you men are in shape, 'cause we gonna be pushing upstream against a current that sometimes is easy and sometimes fast. The lady has a mind of her own. Ha!"

"Wait up! Wait for me!" comes a familiar voice running down the river bank to board.

"Ha! Look who's joining up and heading back?" grins E.J. "You gained some sense, too!"

Army veteran and friend Private John Smith, with a leather satchel draped over his shoulder, steps on the plank and runs up and on board. "Well, not exactly." Then he whispers, "I'll tell ya later."

"I thought we were missing somebody, Colonel," comments Nine Eyes, looking over his list of names. "Okay, that's all of 'em. Let's go."

Cutting diagonally east across the Ohio River toward the new state of Kentucky's shoreline, five men on each side of the keelboat walk to the bow with their long poles, jab the poles into the bottom of the river and walk to the stern, pushing the vessel into the five-mile-an-hour current.

Topside, the cock of the walk is Colonel Pflueger, wearing a derby-style hat with a turkey feather stuck in the side, controlling the rudder. Three other loaded keelboats with passengers head upstream with Pflueger's for safety reasons.

That night at the campsite along the river, thirty tents are staked for the four keelboat flotilla population, and small fires are built.

"I don't know, Charlotte," begins E.J., sitting down in front of their tent opening, "seems like we just did this whole routine with big Mike Fink coming down river with the Pennsylvania militia. It's just not as exciting."

"Oh, it will be exciting to see family and some familiar faces when we get back to Fort Pitt and home before the snow flies this fall," converses Charlotte.

"People we love and other men and women that came down river with us aren't alive anymore, Charlotte. I wonder, did they give their lives in vain?"

"Honey, you'll feel better the farther away from Fort Washington we get."

"Hey, you two," greets Private Smith. "Like I was telling you, E.J., while we were poling, I'm just going as far as Maysville. General Wilkinson has a special delivery that I need to give to someone there."

"How do you get these assignments, Smitty? You're always around these General types," asks E.J.

"Guess they think they can trust me. And look at this face," says Smith turning his head sideways. "How could they not trust this mug? Hee Hee. How could they not trust this face?" Smith continues, grinning. "No really, I don't ask questions. I just do what they tell me. It's pretty easy. Both Generals Harmar and St. Clair have gone back east, and they just passed me onto General Wilkinson. Gotta admit, though, Wilkinson is a little strange. I walked in on him speakin' to someone in Spanish the other day. He went to English real quick, like he was hiding something."

A couple of nights later at another campsite farther up the Ohio, Nine Eyes, carrying a metal candle lantern, walks by Bobby and E.J. and asks, "How 'bout you boys joining the Colonel and a couple of us in a friendly poker game. We always need some fresh blood. Ha!"

"I've played a little with the packhorse fellas. Yeah, sure, why not? I've been lucky before," agrees E.J.

"Can't, I have guard duty first shift tonight," responds Bobby, "but I'll say somethin' to Smitty."

"No, now don't bother the soldier," frowns Nine Eyes. "I just saw him nodding off in front of his tent."

"I'm going to tell Charlotte I won't be too late. Watch closely around her and Phillip for a while tonight though, will ya, Bobby?" requests E.J.

After a few hands at the poker game, the men get comfortable.

"Call me Plug, boy," smiles the middle-aged Colonel Pflueger, dealing cards to four other polemen and Nine Eyes. "We're all friends here. How 'bout 5-Card Stud? One-eyed jacks are wild this time. You savvy, boy?" asks Plug, glancing at E.J. as he deals.

"You've been pretty lucky, kid. You suckering us in?" says Nine Eyes, cocking his head at E.J.

"No, no. I just play what I get."

"I don't see you a-drinkin', kid," observes Plug.

"Grab that rum jug over there, E.J.? Is that your name? E.J.?" requests Nine Eyes. "This whiskey bottle I have is a dead soldier."

"Have some more, boys, and pass it around," orders Plug. "It's just as good as the hooch, and there is plenty of it."

E.J. gets up from the game table to grab the rum container outside the circle of lanterns illuminating the card play area and bumps into Pflueger's wife.

"Excuse me, ma'am," E.J. says with his eyes glimpsing the larger, backwoods river woman.

"Pluggy, come here, sweetie. This is my wife, men. Ain't she pretty?"

The men nod politely while staggering slightly as they get up from their seats. Not totally convinced of the beauty, they sit back down.

With one card down and one card showing, the bidding begins. A couple rounds go by, and E.J., bidding last, raises substantially. A couple of men fold, then Plug looks over at Nine Eyes.

"You eyeing my pretty wife, Nine Eyes?" Plug, not waiting for a response, pulls out a muzzle loader pistol. "Cause if you are, you a dead man. You understand?"

"Don't even think about it, Plug," responds Nine Eyes, "b'cause there's one pointed right back at ya."

"If I catch you anywhere nears her, we prob'ly both gonna be dead," warns Plug, laying his pistol down. "I call ya, E.J. What ya got?"

"I have three kings," replies E.J., exposing two kings and the one-eyed jack of spades.

"I don't think so, little man. I have two aces and the same wild card. I think you been cheatin' all night," accuses Plug.

"Let's see your boot, Plug," interrupts Private John Smith coming in from the dark outside the lighted circle.

"What you getting at, soldier?" asks Plug.

"I think you're the cheater."

"The only boot you gonna see," snarls Plug, getting up and stepping toward the approaching Smith, "is in your face for accusing me of cheatin'!"

Plug takes a wild kick at Smith's face but the private grabs his foot and flips him backward, landing him on his back.

"Hey, soldier boy!" says Nine Eyes, leaping at Smith and landing a punch on the side of Smith's jaw.

"Break it up, break it up!" yell the men getting up from the card table.

"Why, you dirty rat!" shouts E.J., jumping on Nine Eyes's back and choking him in a headlock.

"Get off me, you punk!" commands Nine Eyes, starting to spin around.

"I'll punk you!" retorts E.J., hanging on with one arm and rubbing his knuckle into the top of the riverman's head with his free fist.

"You get off him, you little pip-squeak!" yells Mrs. Pluggy while swinging a metal lantern.

Instead of E.J., the lantern strikes Nine Eyes, collapsing him quickly from the weight of E.J.

"Put that lantern down before you kill someone or start a fire!" demands a poker player, grabbing Pluggy with the help of two others and removing the lantern from her grip.

Private Smith, rubbing his jaw, places a foot on top of the flattened Plug.

"I saw this gizzard take a card from his boot and slip it into his hand," proclaims Smith. "Check this out!" shouts Smith as he removes a boot from Plug and turns it upside down.

This game's over," declares a poker player, watching cards flitter to the ground. "Divvy up the money, boys. It's the only fair way."

"And I'll tell you what, Mrs. Plug," announces Smith, strolling toward the wide-eyed woman, "When these two wake up and want a piece of me, tell 'em I have two guns with their names on 'em, if you know what I mean. Besides that, you're a very nice lady," smiles Smith.

Then, walking away, Smith looks back for E.J. "Come on, lucky."

Chapter 5

1792 – 1793 — Kekionga, the Grand Glaize and western Ohio (Present-day Fort Wayne, Indiana, and Defiance, Ohio)

Two hundred Native Americans walk and ride bareback carrying hunting weapons northeast of Kekionga on the east side of the St. Joseph River. They cross the river just past where Cedar Creek merges with the St. Joe and continue along the west side. Some braves that live along the river in smaller villages join the single-file procession, not for battle but for big game animals to be hunted.

"We cannot go to the Grand Glaize without food," says Little Turtle as he leads the tribesmen, along with Shawnee Chief Blue Jacket and Delaware leader Buckongahelas. "We are not beggars."

Blue Jacket agrees, speaking in the Algonquin language, and continues walking farther north as Little Turtle stops. Half the natives follow Blue Jacket while the rest halt behind Little Turtle and Buckongahelas.

"We've hunted this land before," relates Little Turtle. "You know the targeted meadow north and west of here, Blue Jacket. We start our encirclement now!"

Little Turtle and Buckongahelas head west, leading their group of 100-plus subordinates who have been trained since they were young to know instinctively how to signal and space themselves out.

An hour goes by as the two-mile circumference of Indians connects. Each native can see a brother on either side of him to signal movement for the enveloping encroachment to the kill zone.

Unaware of the braves closing in on them, dozens of white-tailed deer and a few black bears, coyotes, wolves and smaller game scamper or sprint away from the natives but toward each other as the human noose tightens.

Close enough for a sure shot but far enough away to avoid shooting each other, the natives terminate their advancement.

Little Turtle raises his musket slowly to take the first shot and thus to commence the firing.

BAM!

A white-tailed buck goes down followed by other animals as the ring of muskets being fired off from the circle's perimeter bring desired results. Some surviving animals out of panic run past the bow-drawn natives and escape the kill. This does not disappoint the braves as they know the reproduction to follow will bring more food.

After the last shot is taken or arrow projected, the leadership raise their hands, signaling to cease the discharging of weapons.

"Let us give thanks to Kitchi Manitou for providing us with our bounty," offers Little Turtle while the last wounded animals are put out of their misery by the hunters.

The men surrounding the fallen animals stand still with their arms extended upward or kneel with head bowed and commence a chorus chant that has a special meaning of reverence and thankfulness to the Great Spirit for the wildlife that was provided for consumption.

Several minutes pass by until the feeling of thankfulness diminishes. The hunters naturally begin disembowelment of the animals, and any part not to be consumed is removed.

Horses brought along are draped with mostly deer and a few bears and wolves. But the big surprise is the two rogue buffalo that were killed. The sight of the once plentiful bison in this part of the world is now rare.

Back at Kekionga, British fur trader John Kinzie examines Morning Bird's items that Running Deer gave her to trade for ammunition. Recognizing the squaw, Kinzie inquires, "Your friend knows what's going on. Is everyone heading to the Grand Glaize?"

Intercepting the question, "Kinzie, I told ya it was happening," says Antoine Lasselle. "Haven't you noticed the natives packing up? Let this pretty young girl get to where she needs to go."

"The braves are on a hunt, John," inserts Henry Hay. "We'll all be leaving shortly after they return."

Algonquin, English and French languages fly around in one fifteen-second conversation as Kinzie, now resigned to the fact they all will be leaving, continues the discussion. "At least we will have the river current carrying us down the Maumee rapidly because of the rains we've had. But we just got reestablished at Kekionga. Maybe I could live by Tah Cum Wah and Richardville on the St. Marys River?"

"You mean the Kettle River?" asks Hay.

It's the same river," clarifies Kinzie.

"Chief Richardville, with his half-blood French heritage, might be able to pull it off being as they've established the portage to the Wabash," reasons Lasselle, "but if the Americans find you here, John, they'd skin you alive."

"Yes, I can see that happening," responds Kinzie, "but are we sure the Americans are coming here?"

"This is the Indian capital of resistance," reasons Lasselle in French, "and from American military prisoners the natives have taken, a fort at what Washington calls the Miami towns is the ultimate goal."

"Richardville has been advocating peace among the tribes' leaders," adds Henry Hay, "and with Tah Cum Wah being Little Turtle's sister, the Americans will probably leave them alone in hopes of a peaceful solution."

"But moving to the Glaize to get closer to British support only sounds like more trouble," expresses Kinzie.

Meanwhile, in western Ohio, Indian raids take place.

"Come on, we have to move more quickly before that packhorse train gets to the American fort!" coaxes Ottawa Chief Turkey Foot, leading his fifteen braves to attack a supply caravan closing in on Fort Jefferson.

"There they are," informs Bad Bird, halting twenty-five yards into the forest parallel to the trail. "That captive was telling the truth. He was a good scalp, too," remarks Bad Bird to Turkey Foot.

"Amazing what fear does to a white man," acknowledges Turkey Foot. "Pick out the American you want to take out," orders Turkey Foot.

"Wait a second, the pack train has an escort. We'll eliminate them first but let's stay on one side of the trail to attack and leave the packhorse drivers a chance to run."

Spreading out in the forest and moving single-file a safe distance from the supply train, the warriors wait for Turkey Foot to commence the attack.

BAM!

Then a staccato of shots from the natives take down the horseback-riding militia. As predicted, the first volley forces the packhorse leaders and followers to scurry away, surmising the supplies they usher are not worth dying over.

"Finish the wounded off. Grab the horses!" orders a charging Turkey Foot. "Some whites have not run far. Bad Bird, cover our escape!"

"I see that!" yells the anticipating Bad Bird as he reloads his musket and makes sure his pistol is primed, as well.

Two horseback militia burst out of the forest from the opposite side of the trail and shoot at warriors pulling deserted American packhorses by the reins.

"Move quickly, brothers!" encourages Bad Bird, taking aim and squeezing off a musket ball that strikes down a Kentucky militiaman and forces the other to retreat a second time.

Bad Bird darts in to slice through the scalp of the fallen Kentuckian with his knife. "Ha," he chortles while speaking under his breath, "another British reward when I get back to the Glaize."

A hundred piroques and canoes paddled by Native Americans and led by Little Turtle ply northeast with the current on the Maumee River carrying disassembled wigwams, food from the hunt, clothing, supplies and American prisoners from Kekionga.

Passing the Bean Creek outlet on the left that empties into the widening Maumee, the Indians notice acres of cornfields, gardens, wigwams, cabins and local natives watching and waving at them from the banks.

The last few miles of the trek to the Grand Glaize remind Little Turtle of Kekionga, and a touch of melancholy saddens him. He has been on this sector before and now advances his fellow tribesmen and women toward the mouth of the Auglaize River on the right. Making the turn up the Auglaize, he guides the native armada to the north bank for a landing.

Running to the arrival are numerous Ottawa, Chippewa, Wyandotte, Mingo and Cherokee who either call the Grand Glaize their home or are visiting.

"Welcome Little Turtle, Blue Jacket, Buckongahelas!" shouts a pleased Black Hoof, a chief of the Shawnee in this area. "Welcome everyone. You must be tired from your journey. Please, come to our main campfire. Eat what you wish. We have blankets to warm you if you need that."

The reverence for Little Turtle by the greeters is apparent by the quiet and admirable approach the Glaize natives make toward the Miami war chief. After all, he is undefeated against the Americans, with the fabled stories of his victories in 1780, 1790 and 1791 preceding him wherever he goes.

"Thank you," responds Blue Jacket, far more excited than Little Turtle, who instead turns to make sure his displaced people land safely along the bank and the elderly are carefully removed from the boats.

"We have a few captives," states Blue Jacket. "Where would you like them, Black Hoof?"

Watching them depart the canoes, Black Hoof signals for a sub-chief and answers, "They may as well stare at the pole they will die at."

The chieftain leads the tethered whites through the arriving greeters to a lean-to fifteen yards in front of a post with ashes surrounding it. Two of the five captives from Kekionga collapse to the ground sick with fear when they see a prisoner being shaved and painted black.

A few minutes pass by as the last of the watercrafts arrive at the Auglaize landing.

The many diverse tribes gathered chatter in French, the more common Algonquin language and communicate with the use of sign language.

"Is this everyone, Chief Buck?" asks Black Hoof.

Buckongahelas, checking on his Delaware tribesmen, answers, "More are on their way by land using the Detroit trail, bringing horses and further belongings."

"Little Turtle, when we are done here today, your people may set up your village, if it pleases you, on the north side of the Maumee near the Bean Creek mouth," offers Black Hoof. "In fact, a rock seat has been carved and placed in a location there where you can privately meet in council."

Little Turtle nods his approval.

As the elders turn to escort a few of the new arrivals to the campfire, the younger greeters step forward.

"Chief Little Turtle, welcome!"

Little Turtle turns to the voice and recognizes the young warrior.

"Tecumseh! Hello. It is good to see you at this place. We need the young leadership you offer."

"What great victories we have had over Harmar and, most recently, St. Clair!" declares Tecumseh.

Walking toward the campfire, Little Turtle extends his arm around Tecumseh. "I praise you for the training you gave our young warriors back at Kekionga a couple years ago, as well as the scouting that led us to a victory over St. Clair's army. Hopefully, your services have paved the way to peace with the Americans."

Frowning from Little Turtle's last statement, Tecumseh shakes his head. "We will only have peace when there is no white man around that is alive."

Pausing to change the subject, Little Turtle asks, "How are your brothers? Well, I hope."

"Sauwaseekau will be joining us soon. Tenskwatawa lives along the Wabash and is doing well, last I heard, despite the whites being invasive.

But the one who raised my brothers and I after my father died was killed."

"You mean, Chiksika is gone?"

"Yes, Chiksika."

"I am sorry. He was a fine Shawnee warrior. What happened?"

"More white invasiveness, this time down in Tennessee, took his life," responds a grimacing Tecumseh. "Revenge is now my mantra."

A few days later, a large powwow at the Grand Glaize is assembled.

Hundreds of gathered Indians of various tribes circle the twenty pounding Native American drummers. Braves and squaws, young and old—hopping on one foot then the other, spinning, kicking a leg out, all in freelance rhythm—parade around the percussion center.

"I like it," exclaims British sympathizer Simon Girty to Alexander McKee, gazing upon the festive activity from outside the perimeter of seated onlookers passing a calumet.

Girty's words are barely audible above the drum beat, bells and chanting that echoes across the Auglaize River.

"Not only that, Girty," replies McKee, "but the widowed squaws around here are very friendly."

"Forget about that for now, McKee," demands Girty, taking another swig of rum from his jug. "William Wells is here at the Grand Glaize talking to war chiefs. Wells has flipped and is advocating that a peace deal be made with the Americans. Did you know that?" Girty continues, "Wells' white blood and relationship to Little Turtle carries some influence, McKee. We can't let that happen. Thank goodness some British officers are here to back our promised word of helping resist any American army."

"Speaking of the devil," nudges McKee. "There's Wells over by the river, standing by that cottonwood. Let's pay him a visit."

Seeing the British Indian agents and backwoods traders approaching, Wells, knowing the danger he is in, bounds down the river bank for a canoe and paddles away.

Through the dimly lit dusk of night, he propels swiftly by the newly married Running Deer and Morning Bird, canoeing through the waters of the Auglaize in the opposite direction.

"Black Snake, hey, Black Snake!" calls Running Deer.

Powering a confiscated canoe, McKee and Girty paddle by the same couple and close the gap on Wells. "Black Snake? Ha!" chides a smirking McKee.

Glancing at Running Deer and Morning Bird, Wells dips his paddle from side to side more rapidly after hearing McKee.

"They sure are in a hurry," expresses Morning Bird.

"Yes, Black Snake is usually friendlier than that," replies Running Deer as the canoe they are riding in deftly slides into the shore of the Auglaize riverbank in front of the tribal gathering.

Now in the middle of the Maumee River, McKee and Girty catch up with Wells. McKee, in the front, grabs onto the evader's canoe but releases as Wells swats him away with his paddle.

Ten yards farther and the two canoes are next to each other. Girty, avoiding Wells' wild paddle swing, leaps into Wells' canoe, with the momentum tipping both of them into the murky water.

McKee, to this point thinking they just wanted to talk, pulls his pistol out to get a shot at Wells, but darkness makes it difficult to distinguish between the men thrashing in the river. The wrestling takes the two underwater for what seems an eternity. McKee stands up in the canoe to get a better look. Suddenly, the canoe violently rocks from the emerging Girty underneath, and McKee falls backward, discharging his weapon harmlessly into the air and smacking back-first into the water.

"Dang it!" gasps Girty, peering around and taking in deep breaths. "Where'd that varmint go?"

McKee rises from under water and reaches for one of the canoes that are upside down. He recognizes Girty and, between taking breaths, asks, "Did you... get him?"

"I don't know."

"Listen, Girty," requests McKee. "Do you hear him? Do you hear him swimming?"

As the two pursuers tread water and glance around, no sign of the fugitive is detected.

Chapter 6

1793 — The Ohio River

"No hard feelings, Plug?" asks Private John Smith.

"Get on board, soldier. Looks like all fifteen of us are here. We gotta get movin' with the other boats!" roars Colonel Plug. "Last night's over."

"What happened last night, E.J.?" asks Charlotte. "And why does Nine Eyes have a bandage around his head?"

"E.J., what did I miss?" inquires Bobby.

"Oh, we had a little disagreement, and let's just say I got lucky, too."

"Tie this rope to the bow post, E.J.," orders Nine Eyes as he tosses it from behind a team of four-horses.

"Yes sir."

"Looks like we get a pull for a while," states Private Smith.

"All the way to Maysville," says Plug overhearing Smith.

Brum bee-dum, brum bee-dum, brum bee-dum, brrrrumm, brum bee-dum, brum bee-dum, brum bee-dum!

"Speed it up, oarsmen. Can't you hear the drum's beat quickening? Look ahead, Lieutenant! If you can't handle that rudder, get someone who can! See where the pilot boat is heading? Trace its path! The Federalist shall not be the boat throwing the barges into disarray!" commands a demanding Major General Anthony Wayne.

A sixty-six-flatboat flotilla heads down the Ohio River leaving the training grounds of Legionville west of Pittsburgh. Most of the rivercraft carry 2000 well-trained United States legionnaires. Accompanying Wayne's army on other boats are horses, oxen, cattle, animal forage, artillery pieces, tents, military equipment, artificers, food, cooks, surgeons and hospital equipment—the latter two to be used on the expected wounded and illnesses from the incursion into the hostile Northwest Territory.

Several hours of navigating the above-normal river water depth goes by.

"Beautiful country, Lieutenant," admires Wayne, "but rather boring listening to percussion all the time. Set up the band in the flatboat behind us tomorrow to help pass the time."

"May be a distraction, sir, and drown out the main drummer. And by the way, I am a lieutenant colonel, sir," corrects the quartermaster, James O'Hara.

"You may be right on both accounts, Lieutenant," offers Wayne, "but I'm the commander, and we'll try it my way until I stand corrected," demands Wayne with a stern look toward O'Hara. "And don't you ever second-guess me again. Just do it!

"Officer, signal ahead to the pilot boat it is time to land and set up camp," orders General Wayne. "Quartermaster O'Hara, your boats better be able to land and dock without damage."

"The artificers who built them came highly recommended, sir. Final pay to those contractors is being withheld until we see performance."

"Good job," commends Wayne. "Now we will see. I told the pilot captain and scout to select a spot with a meadow in order to get some marching in after the tents are pitched as well as some shooting practice."

"Yes, General, good idea," says O'Hara, adjusting to Wayne's personality.

One after another, the sixty-six large flatboats take turns landing neatly in a row on the north bank of the Ohio River after passing the pilot boat.

"Major Burbeck! Over here!" yells Wayne while he steps off his private barge and straightens his black felt-covered bicorn hat.

Yes, General," acknowledges the approaching fort building engineer and artillery commander. "I thought we had a great first day of travel."

"Nice opinion, Major," expresses Wayne while reaching down to brush off his immaculate blue trousers, "but where are the defensive breastworks? Lieutenant Harrison is out there canvassing the forest a half mile in with his eighty riflemen. What if he encounters 1100 Indians like St. Clair did?"

"Yes sir, I'll get a detachment cutting and trimming back the forest and setting up protection walls immediately," pronounces a saluting Burbeck.

While 800 men from the legion's right wing set up camp, the left wing personnel, disembarking their flatboats, carry their tents and belongings to the left.

"Ah, Lieutenant Whistler, just the man I wanted to see."

"Yes, General?"

"You have seen firsthand what can go wrong while serving with Harmar and St. Clair. If you ever see something I am overlooking, do not hesitate to speak up. You hear me?"

"Yes sir."

"Now, we have two hours of daylight to get fires started and supper prepared," informs Wayne, glancing at camp preparations already taking place. "Geez, look at those tents the left wing is putting up. Crooked as hell. We want them straight, facing the river. Have them stake their tents with some pride. They know better than that."

"Yes sir," salutes Whistler before limping away.

"Whistler, come back here."

"Yes sir."

"When they get done with the tents, get them marching close order. They've been sitting on a boat all day," commands Wayne with his eyes darting, taking in details, enjoying every minute of it.

"Lieutenant Clark! You and Ensign Lewis, front and center. Dad burnit, Clark. How did you get to be lieutenant? Straighten your bicorn. Press out your pants! What have you been doing on your flatboat, sleeping?"

"No sir," answers Clark, saluting.

"I don't care if your older brother was a war hero, you have a long way to go," scorns Wayne. "Get the right flank started on shooting practice with targets, and make sure the newer recruits don't shoot themselves! Ha!"

"Right away, sir," says George Rogers Clark's youngest sibling, straightening out his hat.

"Listen, Clark, before you go. This will be the routine at the end of every day as we travel down the Ohio. We will have an officers meeting tonight at 7:30 sharp at my tent to clarify things. Pass the word to each officer."

"Yes sir, General."

"Lewis?" instructs the Revolutionary War hero. "See that the cattle and horses are off their boat and grazing in this new spring foliage."

Meriwether Lewis nods and salutes, then turns to find the animal-carrying barge.

"General Posey!" calls Wayne, sauntering over toward him, "I need a whiskey."

"Me too, Anthony."

"I know you just got your left wing off the boats, but the right wing already has been told, and I want you to organize them the same way. Keep the dragoons, artillery company, the light company, the two infantry battalions and rifle battalion in separate areas while in camp. I want camaraderie within their ranks."

"Anthony, I like that idea," responds Brigadier General Thomas Posey. "We went through a lot together back during the war. Stony Point, Savannah, even killed a few Indians with you in Georgia, but I don't mind telling you, this army is coming along real fine."

"They ought to be, Thomas," says Wayne, sidling up to Posey. "We have had most of these men almost a year now, and they are ready for a fight. Unfortunately, Congress attempting to acquire peace has dragged out the enlistment times that are expiring."

"I'll tell ya what, Anthony," concludes Posey. "Knox sending us down the Ohio tells me a peace settlement, without a fight, isn't likely to happen."

At Maysville, in the newly formed state of Kentucky, Colonel Plug ends the horse tow at Limestone Creek.

"That's it, folks, we're staying here tonight," informs the keelboat captain. "We need to obtain some supplies."

"This is the end of the line for me, Plug," apprises Private Smith, looking up at the colonel manning the rudder.

"Oh yeah, I forgot," says Plug while signaling to Nine Eyes to untie the pull rope. "Settle up with the soldier, will you, Mrs. Pluggy?"

"Surely will," says a smiling Mrs. Pflueger, still shining from Smith's parting comment the previous night.

"Tomorrow is another day," remarks Plug, already licking his lips while glancing up at Daniel Boone's Tavern.

"Here you go, Mrs. Pflueger," says Smith, handing her three silver dollars. "Yes sirree, I got my satchel and I wish you all the best. I have to hitch myself a ride back to Fort Washington as soon as I deliver this parcel to whomever."

"Thanks for your help, Smitty," says E.J., laying his keelboat pole down.

"Stay outta trouble, Lucky," advises a parting Smith, smiling. He gives Charlotte and little Phillip a hug and shakes Bobby's hand. "I have a feeling we haven't seen the last of each other," Smith predicts as he walks up the bank into Maysville.

The next morning near the mouth of Limestone Creek, three packed keelboats with polemen pushing against an Ohio River current disembarks. The fourth vessel sits idle, with passengers looking around for Colonel Plug, Mrs. Pflueger and Nine Eyes.

"I don't blame those three keelboats leaving us here. They waited as long as they thought fit," says E.J.

"I saw Smith leave earlier this morning, just before you got here, E.J., without his satchel, heading down river on a loaded flatboat," informs Bobby.

"I'm gonna miss him," expresses Charlotte. "I felt safer when he was around."

"Don't worry, honey. We'll be okay once we get movin'," encourages E.J. "Now where is that Plug?"

"This doesn't look like a pleasant situation," pronounces pioneer Simon Kenton, leading his horse and other buckskin woodsmen toward an awaiting barge. "What seems to be the holdup?"

"Waiting for our captain," informs a man from E.J.'s group.

"If this is your keelboat ride, you folks are pointed in the wrong direction. West and north is where the action is. Secondly, your captain is asleep with his friends in Boone's Tavern wearing off their hangovers."

An hour later, Plug and companions not seen before stroll toward the waterfront through the busy dock area.

"Let's go, let's go!" orders Nine Eyes, clapping his hands. "Grab those poles!"

"Who are these men with you, Plug?" asks Bobby, watching strangers crawl into piroques and canoes.

"Oh, just some friends that will escort us since the other boats have left already. You know, just for protection. Dad burn, they just happen to be headin' upstream also."

"I don't like it, E.J.," whispers Bobby.

"You heard Plug," assures E.J., "and we have to have protection from Indians. Numbers will keep us safer."

"I'm not worried so much about Injuns."

Two nights go by. But the same routine of propelling the keelboat becomes more difficult the third morning out of Maysville.

"You hear some splashing around last evening, E.J.?" asks Charlotte watching her husband and other polemen walk by to push again.

"Honey, I was sound asleep since Bobby and I've been on guard duty along with the other passengers. Plug's Dalton boys were in charge of guard duty last night."

"Let's move this boat out into the current more," yells Colonel Pflueger, "so our bottom doesn't drag. I think the river is going down some. Receding, you know, from the rains we've had!"

"The only thing going down is this boat, Plug!" yells Bobby.

"What?!" asks Pflueger from up top. "How can that be?"

"We're sinking!" cries Charlotte.

"Dad burn, you're right, Missy, and we're not gonna make it back to shore," declares Nine Eyes. "Pass your belongings to the Daltons, folks. They can get them to shore dry. Oh geez, we're goin' down fast. Quick, get your luggage out from below!"

"Take this, Charlotte!" orders E.J. as he passes items, along with other passengers adhering to Nine Eyes's directive. "Grab our stuff. I can see water gurgling up through some holes down here!"

"Here, boys," requests Charlotte, "take Phillip onboard your piroque as well as this luggage, but be careful, it's valuable family items in there!"

Forty yards from shore, the vessel is dead in the water, and confusion and disbelief overwhelm the passengers.

"I hope you all can swim," wishes Plug as he and Mrs. Pluggy step into a Dalton canoe.

"Bon voyage, ladies and gents," says Nine Eyes, slipping into a piroque, "and pardon my French."

"What do you mean?" questions a passenger standing atop a nearly sunken keelboat.

"Nine Eyes! What are you doing with my brother," yells Charlotte, observing Phillip being dropped off in shallow water and the piroque occupants paddling down river loaded with travelers' belongings. "and where are you going?"

"Get your gun, Bobby. We can't let them get away with this!" shouts E.J.

"Don't try it, kid!" yells Plug from his canoe, pointing his pistol at E.J. as he is navigated downstream by a Dalton brother, "or we'll all come back and finish you off! Ha!"

"Why you dirty, no-good pirate!"

"You fool, Plug!" shouts an angry Bobby. "Why would you sink your own boat?"

"It never was our boat!" retorts Plug. "Ha! So long, suckers!"

Forced to swim ashore, the passengers ease into the water.

"Keep your guns and powder dry as you swim, everybody," orders E.J. "Charlotte, your dress isn't weighing you down is it?"

"I'm okay, E.J." answers his young wife, stroking freestyle. "It's not much farther."

"I never did trust that Nine Eyes," complains a side-stroking former voyager, holding his weaponry high.

"Why, if we ever meet up with them again, they're goners," reacts another.

An hour later, Charlotte, sitting on the riverbank with her arm around her younger brother contemplating what's next, asks, "Is that music I hear?"

All the milling-about former passengers' ears perk up.

"Could be anything, honey," answers E.J. "It's been an hour getting our thoughts together, and we've seen two flatboats going downstream. None of them are interested in our waving and hollering."

"There's gotta be another keelboat heading up the Ohio real soon," declares a lady.

"Doesn't mean they'll take us on," voices a defeated Bobby. "I'm for heading back to Maysville."

"Gallipolis has got to be right ahead. Let's start walking upstream," urges another castaway.

"We better start thinking about food," suggests E.J., "and whoa, that music is for real and is getting louder. It's comin' from around that river bend yonder a mile," E.J. says, nodding northeasterly.

"What do we have here?" inquires three discharged passengers at the same time.

A minute of silence goes by.

"That's one long parade of boats," comments Bobby in awe, "and look at the flags. Those are American flags."

"Start waving and spread out to catch their attention," orders E.J., beginning to take a leadership role. "That's military. I'd recognize that music anywhere. What is that general's name that's supposed to be our savior?"

"Wayne, Anthony Wayne, if I remember right," recalls Bobby.

"None of them are showing they even see us! They're all floating by, E.J.," exclaims Charlotte, "one after another!"

"Man, that's a lot of boats with a lot of soldiers and such," observes Bobby. "Surely one of them will see us and come over."

"There's the last one, and dad burn if it isn't drifting this way!" exclaims E.J. in amazement.

Chapter 7

Late spring/summer 1793 — The Grand Glaize and western Ohio (Present-day Defiance and Fort Recovery, Ohio)

"Who do my eyes see?" asks a grim-faced Little Turtle staring at Antoine Lasselle inside his Auglaize River trader's cabin.

"Come on, Little Turtle, you know exactly who you see. A tired, old Frenchman trying to make a living," responds Lasselle.

"More like trying to stay alive," says Little Turtle, winking at Running Deer walking in next to him. "Last time I saw you, Lasselle, was in Kekionga giving away some muskets and scurrying away from Harmar's army."

"Now you know that's not true, Turtle. I came to the Auglaize a few months ago just like everyone else when we evacuated the Miami towns. And what took you so long to come visit me?"

Pulling out his hunting knife, Little Turtle sneers and says, "You calling Turtle untruthful?"

"I think he is," agrees Running Deer speaking French, coaxing the Miami war chief on.

"Now Chief, put that knife away. You know I can never tell when you are kidding. And your young prodigy isn't helping matters, either."

"Your British friend, Henry Hay, makes better deals," says Little Turtle, placing his knife back into its sheath.

"I think you just like speaking English better than French," says a smiling Lasselle.

"There you go again, Antoine," says Little Turtle, pretending to pull his knife out, "disagreeing with Turtle. You really don't want to live long, do you?"

"Now, now."

"He does have a nice scalp, Turtle," chimes in Running Deer.

"No seriously, you are half right, Lasselle," confirms Little Turtle, "I don't see any French soldiers around here."

"Shall we ask him to the conference meeting at the longhouse tonight, Little Turtle?" suggests Running Deer.

"Yes, it would be good, my friend, if you listen to what is said. Hay and Kinzie will be there, also. It will be important."

At the battle site on the narrow headwater of the Wabash River, Ottawa Chief Little Otter and forty of his braves walk around, trying to avoid stepping on the hundreds of American skeletal remains.

"Some of St. Clair's cannons have been hidden already. It would be good to know where they are and find any others," says Little Otter in Algonquian.

"To think, as one white captive told us, they thought they were at the upper St. Marys River near Kekionga," recalls a brave.

"What foolishness. Did they not have scouts?" questions another.

"I don't know how many escaped," says Little Otter, "but the remains of Americans extend five miles south.

"There is a cannon over here draped with dead whites. I do not wish to touch any of their body parts."

"Use a limb to remove them," orders Little Otter. "We shall take the long gun and bury it near the river."

"If the British help us, they will be pleased to have the big weapons already at this location to bust the American fort walls farther south."

"Little Otter! Look, over there," requests an aging Chief Bear King pointing. "Do I see movement in the forest to the east?"

"You surely do, Bear King! Let's get our horses!" orders Little Otter. "Those are not brothers leaving into the forest. Those are American spies! Let's get them!"

Back in the Grand Glaize where the Miami are camped, hard feelings are stirred.

"Running Deer, I saw the big Indian," says Morning Bird from her clan's campfire. "He walked by after meeting with Little Turtle at his council rock."

"The Chippewa are camped to the north of us on down the Maumee," says Running Deer. My blood boils thinking of this, my wife. It cannot be tolerated. I will bring this topic up tonight at the longhouse meeting where others will be gathered. The Delaware and Shawnee were in Kekionga when this happened, also. If nothing is resolved of satisfaction, I will resolve it myself, Morning Bird."

"Their Manitou is different from ours, Running Deer. Their reasons for indignant behavior stems from an evilness that makes their warrior mentality difficult to curb. Why would such tribes travel hundreds of miles to fight any and all things that don't even affect them."

"The Chippewa believe, and they may be right, that white incursion anywhere will eventually affect them and their land. Some have fought against the French and the British at one time or another. They have experienced the white influence into their way of life. But it is no excuse to abuse our women and satisfy their natural needs. Why do they not bring their families?"

Meanwhile, back at the Wabash River battle site, Little Otter reaches his horse as does fellow Chief Bear King, and in one clean swoop, they mount their bareback horses and ride after four fleeing white spies.

Twenty of the forty Ottawa that have horses join the chase.

Planning as they pursue, "You head south, Bear King, with ten warriors, and I'll take ten with me!" orders Little Otter. "My group will force them toward you."

"They are probably heading for the forts they come from."

"They'll have information if we capture them," advises Little Otter as they split up.

The Americans, heading east, are not sure they were spotted from five hundred yards away, but now, since they hear the chirping sound of Little Otter's fellow Ottawa, they urge their horses into a gallop.

"Ah yi yi yi ya!," calls the warriors, angling the Americans, now in a meadow, to head south.

Two miles of pursuing through streams and dried creek beds, up and over small hills and down through small valleys takes place as the gap closes. Bear King and his warriors suddenly appear ahead of the Americans, forcing a separation of the four whites. Two spies heading east and two continuing a southerly direction use trails twisting in several directions.

"AH YI YI YI YA!" pierces the ears of the easterly riding whites as the warriors are upon them. Jumping from his horse, Little Otter leaps onto a white spy, knocking him off his horse to the ground and landing on top of him.

"Your death would be too easy!" voices Little Otter, holding his knees on the arms and a scalping knife to the throat of the American.

The lead American is soon caught, as well, but puts up too much resistance and is soon tomahawked and scalped by Bear King's warriors. "Let's take this captive to our village," commands Little Otter, "and see what information he obtains."

At the Grand Glaize, the longhouse fills with chiefs of several tribes as smoke from the fire in the center wafts out the three-foot-wide hole in the birch bark-covered roof ten feet above.

Antoine Lasselle and John Kinzie arrive early and stay to the back. Feeling privileged, they watch the Great Lakes region Ottawa Chief Dog appear. Chippewa leaders Turkey Foot and Bad Bird, followed by Erie, Potawatomie and Huron chiefs and subchiefs of importance, all settle in on one side of the longhouse.

Warriors from farther north, the Saginaw and Mackinac tribes, have not arrived to the southern Great Lakes yet and are expected any week.

Running Deer and Henry Hay walk in opposite the main entrance, nodding and flashing sign language to greet various chiefs.

Alexander McKee, along with his friend Simon Girty, the British advocates and Indian sympathizers, sit up front and are joined by traders James and George, brothers of Simon.

Little Turtle and his Maumee valley delegation of Miami, Eel River, Wea and Piankeshaw take their place across from the Great Lakes leadership. Shawnee Chief Blue Jacket and Black Hoof enter, leading in a Mingo group that had come from the east.

Buckongahelas of the Delaware enters painted for war, making it clear his position against peace.

The Wyandotte's Chiefs Crane and Leather Lips, with their entourage, fill in more of the limited space.

Little Turtle, as the leader of the confederation, stands up to begin the meeting and waves in Chiefs Black Tree and Dirty Face of the Kickapoo. The British officers already seated move over to make room for them.

Murmured French, English, Algonquin and Ojibway fill the room. When Little Turtle raises his arm to speak, quietness pervades and sign language halts.

"Welcome, my brave brothers. I call you brothers despite the fact that some of our tribes at one time or another have met in battle. We unite in peace with each other, with one single purpose to this meeting.

"The army of the white Chief Washington is floating down the Ohio River as we gather here. Many of you are anxious, as I am, to stop this force of Americans and end their desire to take our land from us.

"Some of you want peace without warfare. I do not question your judgment. You have your reasons.

"Some of you think warfare will bring permanent peace. But there are various factors we must consider. Some of you gathered here have defeated the Americans in battle. Some gathered here," continues Little Turtle, glancing at the British and some natives, "have experienced the point of the Long Knives' swords.

"My questions and yours need to be answered before any more blood is spilled. For one, what continues this endless white infiltration from the east? For a decade now, we have seen the Americans flowing into our land, settling on both sides of the great Ohio River. Nothing seems to totally stop their migration into our land.

"We have fought them. We have ignored them. Some brothers have signed treaties with the Americans only to have it broken by one side or the other. We have aligned ourselves with the British or the French in the past. Some brothers fought alongside the Americans during the great war against the British.

"There is something about these Americans that drives them into our land. What motivates them to come back even after the devastating defeat they were given at the upper Wabash?

Many of our brothers bragged that the Americans were finished and would never come back to the Miami rivers. I heard it twice! They now have four forts extending north from the Ohio River!

"Our warriors at the Wabash filled dead Americans' mouths with dirt as a warning sign to any land-hungry whites venturing into our land! "Yet," Little Turtle continues, pausing and lowering his voice, "my brothers, we see another army under the direction of a General Anthony Wayne. Our spies tell us of many soldiers in colorful hats and uniforms. They tell us of many horses and cattle. They tell us of many cannons and ammunition. This only means they seek permanence in our land."

Little Turtle turns toward the British officers sitting nearby. "Can our British allies assure us of redcoats fighting next to us? Can our English friends assure us they will bring cannons to knock down the walls of the American forts?

"Stand up, our British guests!" commands Little Turtle. "Back up the words I continually hear from Mr. Girty and Mr. McKee!"

A scarlet coated officer unfolds from his cross-legged position and gathers himself to his feet. Translations and sign language come to a halt in anticipation of the Englishman's words.

Looking around the room nervously, the Brit slowly begins to speak. "I can assure you, Little Turtle and the rest of you, that according to Lord Dunmore and John Simcoe of Quebec, the crown of England will supply you with arms and food as it has been, and in time, with soldiers and cannons."

Reaction from the majority of the tribal leaders is verbal approval, cautious smiles and nodding heads.

"Seeing is believing!" shouts Little Turtle to the officer.
"I have heard many words at my council rock. It is time to speak publicly. Talk to us, Blue Jacket!"

Blue Jacket pops up and begins, "only absolute power will stop the Americans from invading our land! Signing a peace treaty that some Americans have brought forth will only delay the inevitable. We have defeated the Americans at Kekionga and on the Wabash headwaters. What makes these arrogant Americans think they are in a position to barter our land for peace?"

Loud approval roars from two thirds of those gathered.

"I believe our friends Girty and McKee. Now that this brave British officer backs their word, nothing can stop the power of the confederation!" finishes Blue Jacket.

"Speak to us, Chief White Pigeon," orders Little Turtle, as grim-faced Blue Jacket sits down.

"My people in the past have traveled many miles from the north to assist the warriors at Kekionga and the Wabash headwaters. Our villages have not suffered from these whites like you have, but yet, some of my warriors have died. It is difficult to tell wives and mothers of the loss of their loved one at a distance so far away. My people reluctantly urge a peace treaty that would be advantageous to the confederation of tribes."

"No!" shouts a wide-eyed Buckongahelas, leaping to his feet. "Do you not see that these Americans will do to you what they have done to my people? Peaceful Delaware have been clubbed and mutilated by these white devils for only one reason, for being Indian. Bounties are being sought by American rangers for any Indian scalp no matter what tribe, no matter if they are at peace or a warrior. One is the same to them! I am for complete annihilation of the whites all the way to the Alleghenies!"

More approval resonates.

A fellow Delaware from a different region, Chief Big Cat, stands to take Chief Buck's place. After allowing the interpretations and quiet to return, Big Cat speaks.

"William Wells, or as some of you know him, Black Snake, assures us that we can farm and hunt in peace with the Americans!"

Nudging his partner, "Wells is still alive?" whispers McKee to Simon Girty, shaking his head in disbelief.

"If only we allow the Americans to live north of the Ohio a little ways, everything will be okay," pleads Big Cat as those disagreeing moan.

"Wells once fought with us and killed many Americans but now sees differently. Do you not see the endless predicament we are in? Do you not see through these gentlemen over here?" Big Cat says, turning to the British officers seated. "We fight their war for them."

The chief points to and asks them, "How many white scalps have you collected today?"

"Wait a second, Chief Big Cat!" says Simon Girty, gathering himself to his feet. "The British have supplied many chiefs and their tribes in this room with muskets, musket balls, bayonets, warm clothing and supplies to fight these invading Americans. Also, who do you think is supplying much of the food here at the Glaize and the Roche de Bout?"

Waiting to allow the interpreters to catch up, Girty continues. "I think we owe them a debt of gratitude. Don't most of you think that?" asks Girty, extending his arm and pointing to the gathering.

Many in the longhouse hold up American scalps and voice their approval of what Girty requests.

Chiefs gathered watch and listen as Chief Turkey Foot of the Chippewas concludes the meeting for the night.

"I ask you to seek the wisdom from Kitchi Manitou," urges Chief Turkey Foot. "The Americans, out of fear, will not come to the Glaize to talk. They have peace negotiators at Sandusky and want to talk to us at the Roche de Bout."

"I fear for my people's safety, Turkey Foot!" interrupts Running Deer, standing up unable to contain himself while looking at the chief.

"You Chippewa, as some here know, have violated Miami women as well as Delaware and Shawnee while we were away from Kekionga fighting!"

"What? You do not know this!" says Chippewa Chief Bad Bird, rising toward Running Deer in defense of Turkey Foot. "You do not even belong in here, and your accusations are groundless!"

"My squaw is proof enough for me!" shouts Running Deer, leaping and placing Bad Bird's head in a headlock.

Stepping in the burning ambers of the fire, sparks and flames scatter as Turkey Foot and other chieftains attempt to break up the scuffle.

Out the entryway, Running Deer and Bad Bird grapple, kicking up dirt and surprising warriors that have gathered outside the longhouse.

Miami and Chippewa, recognizing the combatants, step in to protect their brothers by drawing knives that glisten from the larger campfire blazing nearby.

"This is not over," spouts Running Deer, catching his breath. "I want the big Indian!"

Spotting and then advancing toward a taller brave standing behind Bad Bird, Running Deer raises his knife and then lowers it as Little Turtle approaches with his raised arm.

Walking between the opposing blade-wielding Chippewa and Miami, Little Turtle asks, "Do we forget who our real enemy is?"

Chapter 8

Late spring/summer 1793 — Ohio River and western Ohio

"Where's your luggage? What are you folks doing along this river?" asks Lieutenant Tinsley, the commander of the rear guard flatboat of General Anthony Wayne's floating army.

Not waiting for an answer, Tinsley yells, "Hurry up, polemen! Get us back out into the current. I don't know what made me want to come over and get you folks. Why, if Wayne knew I was doing this, I'd be flogged to death."

"We all are obliged, officer," offers E.J.

"Yes, Lieutenant, thank you," chimes in Bobby. "How far are you going today?"

"I'd say past Maysville," answers Tinsley, as he points the rudder man in the direction to the current. "At least that's usually what Wayne plans. Staying away from crazy wilderness towns."

"E.J.?" asks Charlotte, sitting next to her husband on a barge bench seat.

"Yes, Charlotte?"

"It took us quite a few days to get to this spot with all the troubles we've had, and now we're going the opposite direction. Is God trying to tell us something?"

"Well now, Charlotte, I've not heard you talk like this before," says E.J., gazing at his wife.

"I've had time to clear my head and think about things. I mean, we've got some time invested in this land. The Northwest is pretty much all little Phillip here has known," expresses Charlotte, placing her arms around her brother. "What if my mom and dad did survive that battle?"

"I see where you're coming from, Charlotte. Besides that, except for the money we got on us, Plug and Nine Eyes robbed us clean."

"E.J., there's an awful lot of people comin' down this river. Maybe Cincinnati is our home."

At Fort Washington, newly appointed Brigadier General James Wilkinson swigs a whiskey and paces the floor in front of two of his officers.

"I should have been given this legion assignment. Wayne doesn't know anything about leading a huge army. Dang, Horatio Gates, back in the war, was far better than Wayne and Washington put together," rationalizes a complaining Wilkinson.

"Colonel, I mean, General, you've been out here ever since the massacre. You've kept things together while St. Clair and Harmar come and go dealing with their inquiries back in Philadelphia. If anyone is qualified, it would be you," says a supportive Major Thomas Cushing.

"Thank you, Major. Here, have a refill."

"Yes, thank you, sir"

"Personally, I think Washington is in over his head," says Wilkinson, disgusted and intoxicated. "Dang, if it wasn't for French help and General Gates, we would've lost that war. Now here I am, out in this wilderness serving Mad Anthony Wayne. Good night!"

"At least you have control over the 1st Sub-legion, sir. That's the next step to taking over if something happens to Wayne," encourages Captain Isaac Guion.

"Hmmm, yes, if something happens to Wayne," responds Wilkinson. "There is a lot of danger out here. As for the 1st Sub-legion, let's keep them sharp. We've had them here a couple of months waiting on Wayne to arrive. Keep drilling them. They must look sharp during guard duty. Make sure their uniforms look good and the troops are in high spirits. Now I need to dismiss you, but we have to prove we're better than that dad-burned Wayne."

"Yes sir, and thank you for the drinks," replies Major Cushing.

"Maybe some supplies coming down the river can come up missing, Captain," suggests the brigadier general.

"Ah, yes. I understand, sir."

"Now you men are dismissed. I have some work to do before my beautiful wife and Wayne arrive any day now."

After the office door shuts, Wilkinson's thoughts turn to nonmilitary business.

"Now where is my code book?" he mutters to himself. "I can't let anyone else find that. I have to practice my Spanish. Why do those Spaniards pay me in silver dollars? I have to find something quiet to keep all these coins in."

Bam, bam, bam, bam, bam.

Gun shots are heard by the occupants of Lieutenant Tinsley's flatboat floating by the legion camp. General Wayne has challenged four rangers, who just happened to be patrolling the river as the legion landed for the night, to a shooting contest.

"Man, that's good marksmanship! Ha!" laughs Wayne, marveling at the targets being knocked off with rare misses by the rangers and legion's best sharpshooters.

"If the redskins are spying us right now, Anthony, I'd think they would want to sign a peace treaty without further discussion," offers a smiling General Posey.

"If they would sign, Thomas," responds Wayne, "it would be a waste of a dad-burned invincible army."

"Over here, folks," orders Tinsley to his castaways.

"You do more than just dislodge flatboats, don't you?" asks William Henry Harrison.

"Lieutenant," Tinsley answers smiling, "we have some new recruits. At least, that's what I gathered coming down the river the last three hours.

"Just in time. We have men in the legion whose enlistments are expiring."

"They've got experience. Some have been out here since 1790 with Harmar and doin' packhorsing. They're of age and reach the five foot five height minimum, I'd say."

"If not, we'll get some boots on them," says Harrison, smiling.

"I've got a question," speaks up E.J. "Are my wife and little brother-in-law allowed to come along."

"Not happy about it," responds Harrison, "but we have some family with us we've put to work."

"I have another one. You're not much older than Bobby and I. How'd you get to be a lieutenant already?"

"Good question. I like that in a man. The Indians wiped out St. Clair's officers, and my father signed the Declaration of Independence. Any more questions?"

"Ah, no sir."

"Where in the world have you been, Wells? It's been almost a year!" asks a surprised Rufus Putnam greeting the American spy and peace negotiator into his Fort Washington office.

"It's a long story, but here I am, General. I came back. I am a man of my word."

"So this is William Wells?" asks Northwest Territory veteran Lieutenant Colonel Hamtramck, dabbing his head with a cold rag to fight off a fever. "It will be interesting to hear what Black Snake has to say."

"I hope nobody recognized you when you came in," notes Putnam.

"People don't trust you, Wells. I was beginning to wonder myself."

"You took some family members of mine? How are they?" inquires Wells.

"They are still in custody."

"I need to see them."

"Sure, but it's not that easy. General Wayne is going to want to interview you and hear what you have to say. You better be truthful, too, or he'll have you shot. You killed a lot of kinfolks to people here in Cincinnati. Why, if they knew I had you here once and let you go, they may shoot me, as well."

"Listen, Wells," interrupts Hamtramck, "as soon as we debrief you, you'll be heading to the Roche de Bout. We want you to push for peace, but we have to know as soon as possible if the Indians reject or agree to treaty offerings from the United States."

"I get what you want, Colonel. I can tell you right now there are more warriors on the way to the Grand Glaize. The British additions may make the confederation force over 2000. What's the legion have, 3000? From what I see here—"

"That's enough, Wells. What you see here is privy only to us. If you double-cross us, just remember, we have your family and we know where your brother is."

"Honestly, General and Colonel Hamtramck, you think Indian spies aren't watching your every move?"

A mile west of Fort Washington, along the Ohio River, next to Mill Creek is the legion staging area set up by Anthony Wayne as he waits for Philadelphia to order an advance north.

"Ben would be impressed with this camp, Bobby," says E.J., eyeing the hundreds of troops going through marching and combat drills.

"So would your Uncle Ike," expresses Bobby during a marching respite. "This Hobson's Choice must have a thousand tents."

"These uniforms and hats they gave us are nice but I miss the buckskins."

"Don't throw'em away, buddy. Harrison thinks they may use us as guides or scouts."

E.J. covers his ears as a band playing drums, horns and fifes file by led by a color guard.

"Man, I thought Harmar liked military music, but Wayne takes it up—"

"Fall in, men!" interrupts Lieutenant Harrison, shouting at a hundred of the 800-man 4th Sub-legion he is commanding.

"Eyes straight, attention and listen up. The order of attack is scouts, advance guard, riflemen, regulars, dragoons, cavalry and artillery. It may be repetition to some of you, but it needs to be clear to everyone, or there will be fatal consequences!"

"What is he saying, E.J.?" asks Bobby. "Fatal what?"

Harrison continues, "As part of the legion, there is no retreating in combat! If you run from battle, the unit behind you will either shoot, bayonet or put a sword to the coward or cowards! As you have noticed, we are the 4th Sub-legion. We follow the green flag. Your caps, ornaments and uniform facings are green."

"This is getting too technical," whispers E.J. to Bobby. "Just let me fight."

"You dragoons!"

"That's us, E.J.," murmurs Bobby.

"You ride light brown or sorrel horses and carry rifles, sword and pistol. Be prepared to fight from your horse or on foot."

"Man, I like being mobile," says a smiling E.J.

"Okay, mount up!" orders Harrison.

Summer weeks go by, and anxiousness at Hobson's Choice permeates the legion.

"The latest letter from Secretary Knox criticizes the five hundred troops you used to escort the supply train to Fort St. Clair and Jefferson, General," paraphrases General Wilkinson to Wayne.

"Knox needs to turn this whole campaign over to me," retorts General Wayne.

"He goes on to say, your sending that many men north is hurting negotiations with the Indians. That it is too provocative, and one of our negotiators, Tim Pickering, thought he had a treaty all settled until a Simon Girty brought this up."

"Ah, yes. Mr. Girty, that renegade. He watched Colonel Crawford back in '82 get tortured and then burned at the stake by the Delaware," recalls Wayne confidant General Posey.

"Kentucky scout Simon Kenton is friends with Girty," informs Wayne. "Talk about a pair of opposites. Maybe we shouldn't trust Kenton."

"I wouldn't go that far, Anthony. Kenton has had enough of his run-ins with Injuns. He wants this land settled and will be invaluable if we head north," suggests Posey.

"If?" asks Wayne. "It's a matter of time."

"When do you think we'll start leaving, General?" inquires Wilkinson.

"We need to get this supply issue situation under control. You know anything about these contractors Elliott and Williams, Wilkinson?"

"No, no, can't say that I do," responds the 1st Sub-legion leader, "but I can get my officers to look into it."

"Mislabeled barrels have plagued us, and shortages of food. I hate having to buy from these price-gouging settlers that hang a shingle along the river."

"So what does Knox want us to do, keep allowing the supply trains to get massacred and robbed by the Injuns?" asks Posey.

"I'm not going to let that happen, dad burnit," declares Wayne. "And one more thing, shouldn't Lieutenant Clark be showing up with those Choctaw and Chickasaw Indians? He's been on that mission to Tennessee and Kentucky for several weeks."

"Any day now, General," replies Wilkinson.

"That Chickasaw Chief Piomingo served with St. Clair, didn't he, Wilkinson?

"Yes, but I don't know if I'd bring natives friendly or not into this community, General."

"Wilkinson, you're too cautious. I always liked the idea of Indians hunting Indians," conveys Wayne, downing the last three ounces of his hard cider.

Chapter 9

Late summer/fall 1792 and winter 1793 — Roche de Bout, Hobson's Choice and places between

"That's it! We have spent four weeks sitting around in the middle of the Standing Rock River trying to come to an agreement to even talk to the Americans face-to-face at the Roche de Bout," summarizes Delaware war Chief Captain Pipe.

"It is settled," agrees Little Turtle. "You have got what you want, McKee. I better see you and your redcoat friends fighting alongside my braves."

Fifty chiefs wading through ankle-deep water from the half-acre limestone island continue discussions. "You know darn well, Little Turtle, I don't want those Americans in your land, either," says Simon Girty.

"I've seen your son-in-law, slipping around here influencing for peace with those 'land hungrys,' but I can never catch up with him. I think he uses disguises," converses Alexander McKee.

"There are four to five thousand natives coming and going around here. Chances are, he could be here, as you say," replies Little Turtle.

"Twelve tribes united with the Brits is a mighty force, Chief Buckongahelas," boasts Girty.

"We cannot be defeated," speaks the Delaware chief, gazing at the hundreds of Native Americans gathered on the northwest riverbank awaiting the news of war or peace.

Fifteen miles east of the St. Clair battle site, another white captive is being shaved and painted black in preparation for burning at the stake. This village of 150 is one of several that gather information from Americans captured, and the endgame for some is not always pleasant, even when they give it up.

"Cooperate the best you can, and you may not end up like that guy they're painting. What's your name? Sergeant Munson? Is that what you told Turkey Foot?" asks a captive of three years.

"Yes, yes, that's my name. Man, I ca...can't control my bowels," shakes an unsettled Munson. "How have you done it, mister? You are white but not even tied up."

"God's not done with me yet. I've tried to escape twice and have had to run the gauntlet after each one."

"My gosh, why don't they burn you?"

"See that squaw over there, stoking the fire?"

"Yeah."

"She likes me. Her husband was killed by an American ranger along the Ohio while on a hunting trip."

"You've taken his place?"

"It's the Indian way. Just cooperate and pray."

"Okay."

"I gotta go. She's waving me over there. By the way, if I try to escape again and get re-captured, I'll be roasted."

Meanwhile at Fort Washington, preparations are being made to march the legion north on October7.

"You know, the passes the legion has given to visit you this past summer have been hard to get, but we've had a few nights together. Last night, my sweet Charlotte, will have to last us for a while," says E.J.

"I knew the legion would have to move out eventually," says Charlotte, "but I miss you already."

"Come here, Phillip," Calls E.J.

"Yes, E.J.?"

"You take care of your sister, okay?"

"Yes sir, E.J.," says the six-year-old while saluting.

"Something else, E.J.," snuggles Charlotte up to E.J. "I wasn't sure till the last few days, but we're going to be parents. I'm pregnant."

"Holy mackerel, Charlotte! That is, well … you know, I see all these other little kids around here running around, and now we'll have our own," stammers E.J., smiling.

"Yep."

"Now Phillip, you have two to take care of!"

The young married couple embrace into a long kiss and then part, looking into each other's eyes.

"I still plan on joining you, E.J., in a few weeks."

"Until then, you help here, Charlotte. Captain Peirce will be the commandant at Fort Washington while the legion's away. Private Smith says he's going to be escorting supplies to the northern forts once the legion gets things more settled."

Spotting a familiar face, "Hey, Pastor! Over here!" hails E.J. from the main entrance gate.

Ignoring the fort activity, the pastor strides up and remarks, "no one smiles that much when departure is near. My experience tells me your family is getting bigger!"

"Yes. Would you bless us, please?"

The next morning at Hobson's Choice, General Anthony Wayne's legion awaits the signal.

BOOM!

A single cannon fire has Captain James Flinn leading forty horseback spies and guides, including Bobby and E.J., north along Mill Creek.

"This is amazing, E.J.!" says Bobby. "Your Uncle Ike must have had this feeling leading Harmar and us with the cavalry back in '90. How did this happen?"

"It may be amazing, but it is also dangerous. Being a dragoon is one thing, but also serving as a scout?"

"The pay is good, and not too many know the trail much better than us," says Bobby, "except for Flinn. He's been out here since, what'd he say, '81?"

"Yes, '81," says E.J. while glancing around behind him from his moving mount.

E.J. notices the 200 selected woodsmen with axes behind him cutting the trail wider, 200 riflemen fanning out protecting them and the band marching.

"Start playing, conductor. What do you need, an invitation?" E.J. hears a barely audible General Wayne yell.

Looking forward again from his mount, E.J. murmurs to Bobby, "Charlotte will never forgive me if I get an arrow through the heart."

Heading south from the Glaize toward the Great Black Swamp, Little Turtle leads confederation chiefs and 500 warriors to get a firsthand look at the American opposition.

"The water is down, Little Turtle," informs Running Deer, returning from scouting. "I saw a couple buckskin-clad white men riding south away from us through the swamp. They rode a little faster when they saw my spy group close in on them."

"That is an early sign of an advancing army. I am sure they spotted our many numbers. They may be leading us to an ambush," responds Little Turtle.

"Blue Jacket, let's send fifty of your Shawnee and fifty Miami with Running Deer to do some more advanced scouting and to hunt for the evening meal."

"Good idea, Turtle," answers Blue Jacket. "Sending them ahead to scout and hunt this early is good. The autumn sun sets earlier, especially in the thicker forested areas of the swamp."

"There are a few ways of getting through the wetlands, Running Deer, but I want you to follow the Little Auglaize, and we will camp tonight at the larger dune area midway through the swamp," advises Little Turtle.

Running Deer nods, directs his Miami and Shawnee brothers, and gallops off.

The remaining Native American force of 400 advances, riding two-by-two and single file on firm ground between the soft marshes.

Grasses and sparse, scraggly trees protrude from foul-tasting Black Swamp water on either side of the path. Snakes slither through the murky water, and wildcats and an occasional wolf stand in the distance. Thousands of geese and ducks fly above and land in open watery meadows, unperturbed by the Indian presence.

Heading north from 110 miles south of the natives, General Anthony Wayne's first day's march doesn't go perfect.

"Captain DeButts!" yells General Wayne from atop his black stallion. "Get over here!"

Riding up and saluting, "Yes sir."

"Find General Wilkinson, and tell him to move his right wing out farther to the right, for crying out loud. He has to protect the right side of the cattle, packhorses, wagons and artillery. He knows better than that. It makes me wonder if he's doin' it on purpose!"

"Yes sir. Right away, sir."

"Captain Lewis," says General Wayne, turning to another aide-de-camp riding next to him.

"Sir?"

"I want you to ride ahead and tell the axe men the road needs to be smoother and bridges sturdier. If you've looked behind us once in a while, wagons are breaking down."

Lewis salutes and bolts away.

Taking it upon himself, Wayne spurs his horse and busts past the band, ahead of the cavalry and through the fanned riflemen protecting the woodsmen as they widen and better the trail. He arrives next to Captain James Flinn.

Fully exposed to any lurking Indian, Wayne addresses his lead scout.

"Dag nabbit, Flinn. You're not getting paid to parade in column formation. We already discussed this before we started. We need your men out there miles in advance. This will not be another St. Clair massacre."

"You're right, General. Sorry," responds Flinn, signaling his sergeants over to him immediately.

Wayne turns his horse and rides back to find his young aide-de-camp William Henry Harrison.

"Come on, Lieutenant, let's see what's going on in back."

"General, last count we have 3000 troops. Their ammunition is carried on 174 packhorses. You can see several wagons bringing tents and supplies. There's another 100 horses bringing four three-pounder cannons, twenty howitzers and their munitions."

"Now, if Quartermaster O'Hara and our supply contractors do their jobs, each fort along the way will have food and feed waiting on us," adds Wayne.

"Yes sir. The key word is 'if,'" says Harrison.

"The wagons and packhorses seem to be stringing out too much," remarks Wayne. "Not only that, the men on our flanks look tired. Lieutenant, we trained six hours a day in preparation for this."

"We've been suffering the flu, sir," replies Harrison. "A couple hundred men are still at Hobson's Choice. They'll escort supplies and catch up with us when they're healthy."

"I'll tell you this, Lieutenant. There will be no more desertions. Those sick boys better be joining us, or we'll hunt them down. That goes for anyone else."

"Yes, General."

"A hundred lash punishments are not making any difference. Dad burnit, we *hung* deserters at Fort Fayette, and we will do it again if we have to!

"Who is this guy riding toward us, Harrison? I think I'm having a gout flare-up. It's affecting my eyes."

"I believe that is William Wells, sir," answers Harrison.

"Good, I trust him. He's been worth every penny."

"General Wayne, Lieutenant," begins Wells. "I figure 500 natives heading this way through the swamp, which means they have left behind 1000 or more at the Glaize and Roche de Bout."

"Why is that? Why not bring them all?" asks Wayne.

"Their plan is to attack your supply lines, General," responds Wells. "Starve your army and save the main force to finish you off."

That evening at a higher land mass in the Great Black Swamp, the confederation forces consume venison, bear and duck and listen to Little Turtle's stories.

Not letting their guard down, designated Indians walk the perimeter.

"Grey Wolf, show everyone that scalp you have with the ear attached," requests Little Turtle, smiling slightly. "Do you remember where you took that hair?"

"Not sure, Turtle."

"I remember," recalls the Miami chief. "It was a year ago next moon that you, Running Deer and I led an early morning attack at a fort they call St. Clair. Only the whites would name a location after a defeated leader. Ha!"

"Hmm, yes," recalls Grey Wolf.

"Information taken from American captives about that supply train was wrong, but we made up for it with the attack on their camp outside the fort gates," says Running Deer, using the Algonquin language for all to understand.

"We had them outnumbered three-to-one," tells Little Turtle. "Do you see some of those horses tied over there on the line?"

Twenty heads turn toward the horses.

"Many of those we ride come from that packhorse train from a year ago."

"I still don't know why those soldiers inside the fort didn't come out and help the Kentuckians," says Grey Wolf, shaking his head. "Are all the whites afraid? We make a few sounds at night, and they don't come outside the gate for days."

"That was a valuable and large number of supplies we were able to take from the Americans," remembers Running Deer.

"Almost as valuable as the ear scalp. Ha!" laughs Grey Wolf.

"But not as valuable as the scalp of the Long Knife leader called Mad Anthony Wayne," says a grimacing Blue Jacket.

Finally reaching Fort Hamilton at the end of a first day's march, Wayne's legion assembles camp around the stockade. As camp is being arranged, E.J. and Bobby ride in with orders from Captain Flinn.

"Glad there is a flag on top of the tent to let us know where headquarters is, Lieutenant," says E.J., saluting.

"Yes, how is it out there, Carlisle?" Harrison says, returning the salute.

"Just a bit of advice from a kid, but if I'm an Injun and I see a fancy flag like that on top of a tent, well, I know who I'm gonna target." says E.J.

"I know what you mean, but try telling that to the General, and he'll hand your rear end to you. Now, what do you have?"

"We have seen signs of Indians but haven't seen any until now," says E.J., pointing to Lieutenant William Clark riding in with twenty Chickasaw and Chocktaw.

Harrison turns to the entrance of the large tent and calls to General Wayne, "Clark's here, sir."

"Well, it is about time," says Wayne, walking out placing his bicorn hat on and swatting away gnats and mosquitoes.

After initial greetings are made, Wayne offers food to the braves who will be used as scouts and in guerilla warfare.

"Clark, interpret for me," orders Wayne. "Tell Chief Piomingo we appreciate his help, but unfortunately, some in the legion don't trust any Indians. The Americans in this army will be told not to do them any harm."

While Clark speaks Chickasaw to the chief, Wayne turns to Harrison, "Who are these two guys?"

"This is Sergeants Carlisle and Fulton, guides with Captain Flinn."

E.J. and Bobby salute.

"Okay, they need to hear this, too, and have them take the word to Flinn. Wells, Simon Kenton and Major William McMahon are out doing surveillance, and the Chickasaw and Choctaw will be joining them wearing yellow ribbons in their hair and feathers scouting also. Dad burnit, the general order is don't shoot the American Indian scouts."

"I remember Harmar giving that order, too," whispers Bobby to E.J.

Chapter 10

Fall 1793 — The Grand Camp, Fort GreeneVille (Present-day Western Ohio)

In the six days after leaving Hobson's Choice, Wayne's 3500-man legion camps and travels ninety-nine miles with brief stops at Forts Hamilton, St. Clair and Jefferson. Six miles past Jefferson, a camp is established midafternoon with the usual defensive care. Temporary log breastworks at each corner of the encampment are built for protection against Indian attacks. Outside, 200 riflemen patrol the perimeter. Tents are pitched in rows, animals are watered and meals are prepared. Frustrated Native Americans watch from a distance.

"We can't get close to this General Wayne," offers Running Deer, hiding with ten Miami behind a grove of beech trees 100 yards from mounted riflemen. "It's like he never sleeps."

"He is no St. Clair," agrees half-French and half-Miami Chief LeGris, turning to Little Turtle. "Unlike Harmar at Kekionga, a quick victory may not come militarily over an army this alert."

"Blue Jacket, you'll have to agree, patience against an army we can't get a good look at is necessary. Our spies tell us they have many mouths to feed. Let's gather our horses and brothers and get between Wayne and his Fort Washington," orders Little Turtle.

"You underestimate the stealthiness of our warriors, Turtle," remarks Blue Jacket. "We'll get some information, and this time, we will wipe the Americans out all the way to the Ohio."

Fifteen miles east of the legion, white captives attempt to survive at the Ottawa village of Chief Turkey Foot.

"I'll tell ya, Munson, I didn't think you were going to survive the gauntlet," offers the three-year veteran of Indian captivity.

Speaking softly, "That last club about did me in. If that was what it was," Munson says, still disoriented.

Dabbing Munson's injured bruise and gash on the side of his head and other wounds with the edge of her dress, an Ottawa squaw talks to him in Ojibway.

"She speaks of your bravery, Munson. From the looks of the warriors that formed the tunnel, they were impressed, too," says the adopted American. "I may be wrong, but I think she likes you."

"Oh yeah?"

"The shaman have some herbs and root spices to heal you. It will just take some time."

Smiling, the squaw gently strokes Munson's head.

"If you survive, you might get transported to another village or given back to the Americans in a prisoner swap. I've seen it all, pretty much."

"I'd just as soon stay here," wishes Munson. "By the way, how'd you get here?"

"I survived the battle at Kekionga back in '90. Anyway, you won't get to make that decision."

"I didn't figure I would."

"This squaw is a widow and has had choices before. Whites have been rejected by her then died in later gauntlets or were burned at the stake. Sort of depends on battle results."

Two days later, the legion is stationary six miles north of Fort Jefferson.

"Here comes the Kentucky militia, General!" informs aide-de-camp DeButts standing outside Wayne's tent.

Eight hundred mounted militia backwoodsmen ride in four-by-four column formation among the pitched tents and halt in the temporary parade grounds.

"My old friend Charles, it is good to see you!"

"Anthony, glad we caught up with ya," says General Scott, dismounting and at the same time signaling General Todd to have the volunteers do the same.

"Come in my quarters, let's catch up. Have a little rum with me."

"Ooowe!" exclaims the bowlegged general. "A little Kentucky bourbon, I hope!"

"I believe we have that, too. Have a seat."

"I like the way you have your camp protected, Anthony, because we saw plenty of signs of redskins and sighted them too. We had no run-ins with 'em on the way up here, but folks around Cincinnati have had Indian raids and terrible losses ever since the legion left."

"We have men in the legion with kinfolk back there who will not be happy to hear that."

"If their loved ones are in the fort, they should be okay," assures the general.

"To be honest, Charles, it is getting too late in the year to pursue the Injun federation. Animal foliage is near the end for grazing. Our food stockpile is low. I'm leaning toward staying here for the winter and moving on next spring."

"I was wondering, when I got the word to proceed north, how far this campaign would get this fall."

"We have an area for your militia to camp. It is within eyesight of the legion. At least you'll get reports from our scouts while you're here."

"Word in Kentucky is the Indians have got quite a buildup going on."

Wayne stands up and limps around.

"Not only that, but they've been giving our pack trains some problems," says Wayne. "We'll have your boys, on their way home for the winter, escort the packhorses to Fort Washington to load up more supplies."

At a brigadier general's tent, the conversation is different.

"I tell you, Major Cushing, Wayne doesn't know what he is doing. You could run this army better than he is!" complains a pacing James Wilkinson, now commanding the 1st and 4th Sub-legions.

"Thanks for the compliment, but you are the one who should be leading us, General."

"I think the contractors, Williams and Elliott, are doing the best they can to get us food. Wayne's just mismanaging it! I'm going to keep sending correspondence to Secretary Knox," informs Wilkinson, folding a letter. In fact, I have congressional friends circulating an impeachment petition against Wayne."

"Interesting, sir."

"Captain Guion, I like this Private Smith as our courier," says Wilkinson glancing across the table. "He doesn't question anything, and he gets the job done."

"Yes sir."

"Let's send him back to Fort Washington with this batch of correspondence as soon as the next convoy heads out."

Four miles north of Fort St. Clair, a supply train with twenty wagons of supplies and a ninety-man escort traveling toward Wayne's camp is surprised.

"Fire!" commands Chief Little Otter.

"Bam, babam! Bam Bam!" cracks the British Brown Bessie muskets of the Indian coalition.

Little Turtle and warriors leave their hiding places to attack wagon drivers and soldiers not killed immediately. The only refuge for the Americans is to scatter into the forest opposite the charging natives.

"Ahyiyiyiyi!" scream the warriors.

"Otter is right!" exclaims Little Turtle to Running Deer, galloping toward the wagon train unimpeded. "Give them an out, and there are very few brothers lost."

"Eleven Americans down!" yells Running Deer to his subordinates. "Finish them off! Grab the horses that the whites are cutting loose!"

"Blue Jacket!" yells Little Turtle, pointing at easy prey as he rides in, "let's take some prisoners!"

Pushing the Americans deeper into the forest away from the wagons, some resistance from the escort convoy is finally felt.

Little Turtle calls for his warriors to collect their injured or killed brothers and return.

In Philadelphia 570 miles to the east, Secretary of War Henry Knox finishes reading to President George Washington a letter from Brigadier General James Wilkinson.

"I don't hear of any other complaints from the Northwest Territory," responds Washington. "Besides that, no one is paying attention to the warfront this side of the Alleghenies unless it's a wife or mother of a soldier!"

"That is puzzling," conveys Knox. "The correspondence then is usually about getting a loved one freed from desertion charges."

"I never found Wayne incompetent during the War of Independence. In fact, I found him exemplary. Men getting out of control? I have serious doubts."

"General Wilkinson served Gates well in the war. I find it hard to believe he would make things up," retorts Knox. "Congress is taking the matter up."

"Congress? That's a group for ya. Thankfully, businessmen in there and not the politicians have a handle on matters."

Six miles north of Fort Jefferson, at a place called the Grand Camp, decisions are being made after two weeks at the same location.

"Meet me at my tent when we are done, Major Burbeck," requests Wayne from atop his horse to his artillery leader and fort building engineer.

Rain and snow fall on his marching and drilling legion when Wayne finally calls a halt to the activities and rides to his marquee.

Handing the bridle to a private, Wayne shakes his bicorn of collected water and brushes his coat of the moisture. Wayne greets Burbeck and laughs, "Major, did you hear about that snake that crawled into Kentucky General Todd's bedding while he was sleeping two nights ago?"

"No sir," smiles Burbeck. "I haven't been around the volunteers."

"Woke up with it lyin' on his belly! That appeared to be the last straw."

"Ha! The cold blooded animal wanted to hibernate," comments the grinning Burbeck.

"The out-of-control brush fire in their meadow last week before the rain wasn't amusing. I was going to send them back to Kentucky anyway. We'll call them back up next spring. Besides that, we are sending the 800 dragoons to Lexington for the winter."

"Ok sir, how does that affect me."

"The rest of us are staying here! Build us a fort, Burbeck! How do you think it affects you, for crying out loud? There is plenty of forest around here. Put everyone to work. I want it fifty acres in size with six, no, make it eight blockhouses. Build the blockhouses and fortifications first. GreeneVille has to be big.

"Yes sir. GreeneVille, sir?"

"Yes, Fort GreeneVille! Construct enough barracks for 4000 men, six men per barrack, and everything that goes with it."

A few miles away, enemy Native American chiefs converse.

"Blue Jacket, some warriors are going to stay in the Ohio valley with Turkey Foot and continue to starve the Americans with raids," states Little Turtle.

"I have family, Turtle. I need to get back to them for the winter, and I assume you do, too."

"You are right, Jacket. The Glaize awaits me. I am too old to spend these months in the wilderness."

"When we come back next spring," advises Blue Jacket, "do not expect such leniency on the Americans from me, Turtle. When we raid, it will be complete annihilation. No survivors!"

"When we come back, there better be British with us and 1000 more warriors," opines Little Turtle.

"When the British come with us, the cannons they bring will knock down the American fort walls and make it easy for us to defeat them!" "Cannons from St. Clair's army lay hidden around the battle site. The British can easily repair them and find the cannon ammunition concealed as well."

"We have seen many Americans heading south to their forts for the winter. I would imagine Wayne will be, too," summarizes Blue Jacket.

"I am not so sure. This one, who never sleeps, is not predictable."

At the Grand Camp during a break in construction of Fort GreeneVille, soldiers pass the time.

"I tell ya, Bobby, we can make a little extra cash on this guy," whispers E.J. "Just let me do the talking."

"Okay, I'm game, but gambling is not allowed, and I don't feel like receiving fifty lashes from a wire rope whip."

"It's not card playing," reasons E.J.

"You loose, Mac?" says E.J. to his fellow scout and former packhorse driver, Robert McClellan.

"I'm a little sore from chopping trees the last couple days, but let's give it a try."

"This ain't no game, Mac. Pardon my language. You have to dad burn make it!" says E.J., covering his mouth quickly to muffle his words.

"Okay, okay."

"We'll split it three ways since Bobby's going to hold the money," reasons E.J.

"Sounds good to me," says Bobby, grinning.

Stepping away from the two, E.J. looks around at the legion regulars talking and drinking water.

"Listen up, you men!" yells E.J.

"I'll wager each one of you a dollar that my friend here, Bobby Conrad from Pennsylvania, can jump over that team of two horses standing over there! One leap!"

Soldiers, liking a little fun and action, approach E.J.

"That would be a heck of a feat, but you know your friend, and he can probably do it," responds a thoughtful private.

"Okay," answers E.J., "I can understand that. Well how 'bout this older guy. Robert, is it?"

"Yeah, but I don't know," answers McClellan slyly.

Several men step up, and one says, "I'd bet he couldn't make it over one horse. Yeah, I'll bet he can't make it over two."

"Not only can he jump over two, he'll jump back over while the team of horses is moving!"

"Oh, I don't know about that," whimpers McClellan shaking his head.

"If you're in, give your dollar to Bobby and stand by him, out of the way," orders E.J.

Word gets out to a few others gathered nearby, and the stakes get higher.

"Okay, Mac. Don't let us down."

McClellan does a couple calisthenics and walks around timidly to dramatize the moment. He then takes a running start toward the horses and pulls up short.

"Pay up, give us our money!" one guy yells. "I told you he couldn't do that!"

"No, no. He has to at least try to jump, to count as an attempt," shouts E.J. "You want to double your bet?"

"Don't push it, E.J.," says Bobby out of the side of his mouth.

"Yeah," shout several men.

"Okay, see Bobby over here. Come on, Mac—I mean mister! Show these guys!"

Again taking a running start, McClellan leaps and clears both horses with a foot to spare but lands wrong and slightly twists his ankle.

The men moan as Bobby and E.J. cheer the results.

"It's a fix! How did he do that? He's got springs in those boots!" yells a disbeliever.

"Now he's got to do it again comin' back while it's moving!" hollers another.

"Did I say that?" asks E.J., looking at Bobby and then at a limping McClellan.

"The bet's off, Robert's hurt!" shouts E.J.

"Oh no, a bet's a bet," roars an ensign.

Mac walks around trying to shake the injury off and then gives a nod to start the team of horses hitched to logs to start moving.

Running past the observing men and toward the horses in motion, McClellan vaults off of his good foot, and with a scissor-kick jumping style, clears both horses, landing safely.

As the losing bettors stare awestruck in disbelief, the exhilaration of McClellan's successful leap has E.J. and Bobby thrusting their fists in the air with a collective, "Yes!"

A few days later, Simon Kenton, returning with his 120 scouts, rides into an under-construction Fort GreeneVille. Kenton dismounts, observing blockhouses and picket walls being assembled as well as a band marching and playing music in front of General Wayne's flag-adorned tent.

"What's going on, General?" quizzes Kenton through a flapped-shut marquee door.

A moment goes by, then stepping out gingerly because of gout issues, Wayne answers, "Who wants to know?"

Scanning his guards, Wayne bellows, "What's the idea of letting just anyone call for me? That will be ten lashes issued when your duty is over today!

"Kenton, is it? Get in here! I have to lay down!"

"Why isn't this army on the move, General?" asks Kenton. "In one week, you're there scalping redskins!"

"We have a food shortage, Kenton. We're on a single ration of flour and beef per day until more supplies come in, and who are you to question me? Tell me what you and your glorious scouts saw. Did you bring me any prisoners?"

"Major McMahon and I and the rest made it all the way to the Auglaize and Maumee Rivers, General," briefs the frontiersman scout.

"Well, what did you see?"

"Hundreds of warriors, wigwams—you name it, General! More than I'd ever seen."

"Tell me something new, for crying out loud! Are they coming this way?"

"I'd say they are settling in for the winter. It would be a good time to attack!"

"Well, Kenton, that isn't going to happen immediately. My officers can find some tents for you and your men to stay in while permanent quarters are built. Meanwhile, give us a hand at construction."

"General, I'm not in the fort-building business. I'm taking my men back home."

A few days later at Fort GreeneVille, three men stand on a gallows.

"Are those nooses too tight, my sons?" asks the pastor, standing with his Bible next to a military hangman.

"No, it's okay, Pastor," mutters a couple of voices.

"Do each of you know why you are about to die?" asks the executioner.

While waiting for an answer from each one, a full assembly of legion soldiers not guarding, scouting or patrolling the surrounding forests stands in straight rows around the scaffold.

"I shot and killed a man, sir. I told the court martial I was sorry. That heathen Wayne could pardon me if he wanted to."

"That is correct, and you haven't been pardoned. Eye for an eye, mister."

Moving to the next man chewing tobacco and spitting, the executioner asks the same.

"I don't know, you tell me."

"Multiple desertions and recaptures," answers the executioner.

The third man is asked, and getting weak-kneed, his response is desertions.

The pastor steps up in front of the three and asks if they have asked for forgiveness of their sins.

"Have you accepted Jesus Christ ..."

"I'm too young to go, Pastor. I didn't mean to shoot him. I was just mad, dad burnit! I was just mad!" sobs the murderer.

"Have you accepted Jesus Christ as your lord and savior?"

Each of them nods in affirmation.

A lieutenant points to three drummers to commence a drumroll.

Complete silence from 1300 soldiers holding their breath ends when the drummers are signaled to stop. The trapdoors open, and a collective moan is heard from the troops as the convicted fall to their deaths.

Chapter 11

Winter 1793 – spring 1794 — The Grand Glaize, Roche de Bout and Western Ohio Territory (Present-day Fort Defiance, Fort Recovery and Maumee, Ohio)

At two large Indian villages, the Grand Glaize and the Roche de Bout, natives from ten tribes attempt to survive the winter along the Maumee River and tributaries.

Little Turtle and his family share with other families a ninety-foot longhouse tucked in a forest near the river, where they fish and can easily gather wood for burning to stay warm.

"The Ojibway and Ottawa have been existing on our food," says Little Turtle in Algonquin to his clan gathered around the fire in the longhouse. While smoke exits the hole in the cedar-bark roof, he continues. "The British for the most part have kept their promise of bringing us food to compensate for that."

Draped in bear fur and buckskin leggings, Running Deer, always eager for knowledge, walks in the end entrance toward the related families that are gathered. Dropping two skinned beavers and a raccoon near the fire, he speaks. "These were not easy to find, and it is just early winter."

"Thank you, Running Deer," responds Little Turtle and his family.

"How does one survive if there are no animals or fish?" asks Running Deer.

"Living next to the Chippewa this winter does make me somewhat uneasy," begins Little Turtle.

"Tell us more?" inquires Running Deer.

"I'm not saying other natives to this land have not resorted to desperate means to survive harsh winters, but some Ojibway are called Windigoes."

"Why is that?" probes another brave, staring at the fire.

"Long ago, it was common for the giants that walked the earth to consume natives as well as animals. After the giants became extinct, those practices continued when precarious means to survive surfaced. Those Ojibway that resorted to cannibalism were given the Windigo name and were shunned by non-cannibals."

"Much like consuming a heroic enemy to gain their strength?" asks Running Deer.

"It is best to eat a brave enemy's heart while it is still beating."

Captain James Flinn, the lead scout for General Wayne, has paired off his forty men in advance of Major Burbeck's 300-man force heading for the St. Clair battle site.

"Man, Bobby, I like the way Wayne keeps us active, but since Charlotte's bad pregnancy and losing the baby, I have only been with her a few days at Fort GreeneVille."

"I am sorry for the miscarriage, E.J. At least she is nearby and not at Fort Washington anymore. Several families have moved to GreeneVille since it's been completed. There was a couple nice gals I met that are friends with Charlotte, too."

"Dad burnit, we have to keep our eyes moving, Bobby. I'm just glad we get to follow the trail to the battle site while the others are floundering through the forest. Hard to believe it's been three years since the massacre."

"We're beginning to get close, E.J. Even though we've passed through here scouting before, it doesn't get any easier."

"It'd be good to find and bury Charlotte's parents and brother before she comes any farther this way."

"I agree, but these skulls and skeletons are all bashed and unidentifiable," utters Bobby, wincing. "All these broken muskets and American belongings lying around are useless."

"This was the regulars' camp, Bobby. Let's get out of this boneyard and water our horses down at the river."

"Major Burbeck should be along in a couple hours, I'd say, wouldn't you, E.J.?"

"Yeah, and did you hear Flinn say Wayne himself is leading a packhorse train here about an hour behind Burbeck?"

"The general exposing himself to an Injun arrow is either a fool or has a personal vendetta," declares Bobby.

Dismounting their horses for watering allows the friends to stretch their legs. Filling his canteen, E.J. notices round iron protruding the narrow Wabash River surface.

"Hey, look at this," he says, dropping the reins of his horse and walking along the bank.

"That looks like one of the cannons the Indians were said to have hidden after the battle," remarks Bobby, following E.J.

"We need to mark this spot for—"

Suddenly, the watering horses are startled and freely bolt away from the river.

"Aw, nuts. What caused that?"

"Shhh," whispers E.J., pulling his musket to his waist.

"What do you see?"

"Wolfpack," utters E.J. "They've caught our scent."

Out of a clearing, fifteen wolves with their pups cross the shallow river and start howling and circling the two companions.

"We thought Indians was all we had to worry about," moans Bobby.

"Fix your bayonet," orders E.J. "You have your pistol also, don't you."

"Yes."

"Slowly, let's get back-to-back to this tree."

"When you start firing, don't miss, buddy," advises Bobby, raising his musket as the wolves close in.

The boys each squeeze off a musket round, both killing a hungry wolf.

Temporarily scattered because of the musket cracks, the wolves howl, moving in more aggressively.

Ten seconds later, Bobby and E.J. discharge their pistol at the teeth-baring predators, striking two more. Not to be denied, the wolves come back.

Afraid to take the time to reload, the pair ward off the remaining wolves with their attached bayonets. E.J. slips down the trunk of the pawpaw tree, and a growling carnivore rapidly advances. Avoiding the bayonet, the wolf bites E.J.'s buckskin pant leg, pulling him away from the tree.

"Help!" yells E.J., as he unsheathes his skinning knife to defend himself.

Bam!

A musket crack from a distance knocks down the wolf and scatters the others.

"You okay, E.J.?" asks Bobby, unaware of his friend's predicament.

"You shoot that?" quizzes a grateful E.J., scrambling to his feet.

"It's Mac!" answers Bobby, sighting Robert McClellan and his partner on horseback pulling up from thirty yards away and aiming at the relentless wolves.

Bam! Bam!

Gunpowder smoke perfusing the cold winter stillness slowly drifts away, revealing seven dead wolves, four live pioneers and the surviving wolves recrossing the river.

The next day at the battleground, Major Henry Burbeck directs his 300-man detachment to cut down marked trees.

"Major," reminds Wayne, "I want it square at 150-foot wall curtains with blockhouses at the corners."

"Yes sir."

"I want it built around those most concentrated skeletal remains!"

"Sir, we're going to have to move them," advises Burbeck.

"Get the permanent blockhouses assembled first. I want the men to absorb what the redskins have done."

"Yes sir."

Glancing at the riflemen patrolling the perimeter, Wayne walks toward a stunned Captain James Flinn. Wayne interrupts Flinn's introspections and asks, "Are your forty scouts out there spying for us?"

"Yes, General."

"Go join them. Don't let those heathens add our bones to this pile." Walking back toward Major Burbeck, Wayne shouts, "It is Christmas Eve, Major! What better message to send to the Indians than that we are taking back our fallen ground!"

Three months later, eleven miles south of Lake Erie on the Maumee River, a dedication takes place.

BOOM!

"Yes, Chief Little Otter. This Fort Miami will definitely assure you that the British have your back," says John Simcoe, the lieutenant governor of upper Canada.

"I'm impressed but Little Turtle wants to know how many redcoats he can count on this spring against Wayne," asks the Ottawa chief through interpreter Alexander McKee.

"You should expect a couple hundred or more," responds a vague Colonel Simcoe, watching members of the British 24th Infantry and Royal Artillery march back into the fort.

"There better be, what you say, 'more.' And the number of cannons?" pushes the chief.

"There will be some," replies Simcoe.

The colonel turns from Little Otter toward the fort-building engineer, Lieutenant Robert Pilkington, and a conversation turns private.

"Technically, we are on shaky legal ground building this fortification, but Lord Dorchester wants us here until we get further orders," discloses Simcoe.

"We have a strong overlook of the river, Colonel, with easy access to shipping supplies."

"Yes, you've done an excellent job, Pilkington."

"Thank you, sir."

"Listen Pilkington, I fought against Wayne several times in the war fifteen years ago. Between you and me, if he breaks through the natives and what troops the crown gives us, Wayne won't stop here with that reported huge army of his. In fact, I wouldn't be surprised if he bypassed us and went directly against Fort Detroit."

Later in the spring at Fort GreeneVille, during a break in the legion training and drills, General Wayne hosts his generals, several scouts and Captain William Clark in his marquee tent.

"Clark's resistance against the raid on his pack train near Fort Washington indicates the military training is paying off, gentlemen!" brags Wayne standing up to pace around, "I wish our army's resistance to the flu epidemic was as good, but we must emphasize the positive and move forward.

"Sergeant Dold, seated over here, captured two Shawnee, and information from them indicates peace was at hand until British Indian agent Alexander McKee stirred them back up! Tell 'em what else, Sergeant!"

"They've built a fort two miles north of the Roche de Bout."

"Who's they? The Indians?" asks an invited backwoodsman.

"No, the British."

"That's American land."

"It's all American land, you loggerhead!" yells Wayne. "Just another reason to catch and hang McKee, Girty and the whole lot of them!"

Settling back down, Wayne explains. "Here is the situation. Flinn and his forty scouts are out spying and are the first warning around Fort Recovery. Everything has been quiet this winter, but I'm planning on sending Flinn's group north to watch for an Indian buildup.

"Kenton has gone home to Kentucky and I don't know if he'll be back. Ephraim Kibbey is coming up from Cincy this summer with experienced woodsmen. And I expect William Wells back any day with information from the Maumee region.

"Now, Captain Eaton, I want you surveying the waters of the Wabash, St. Marys and Auglaize Rivers. Map it out. Where do the waters flow to from the Great Black Swamp? Find it out!"

Wayne continues with his dispatches. "Mr. Collins, you have a special spy mission. Take fifteen men and see where the natives are north and east of Fort Recovery. Check out a place called Girty's Town.

"Captain Hartshorne, work with Collins and cut a road to Girty's Town.

"All of you, report to Captain Gibson at Fort Recovery any knowledge you acquire. I don't care how unimportant you think it is. His garrison is at the trigger point. Meanwhile, we are accumulating supplies and training up for complete victory this summer!

"Men," commands Wayne, staring at General Wilkinson, "I want no one undermining this campaign."

Then turning to view the assorted scouts, Wayne concludes, "It is very simple. I want information, and I want scalps!"

Chapter 12

June 1794 — Western Ohio Territory, the Grand Glaize and Fort Recovery (Present-day Defiance and Fort Recovery, Ohio)

Fifteen miles east of Fort Recovery, Captain James Flinn commands his forty scouts who are paired off, moving easterly, traversing trails, meadows and forests.

"Hold up, Bobby," cautions E.J. to his partner fifteen feet away. "Dismount, and get down."

With his vision blocked by several trees and underbrush, Bobby crawls to E.J.'s side. "What ya' got? Oh, geez," sighs Bobby, eyeing the danger.

Angling fifty yards ahead of the young scouts on a diagonal trail are twenty Ottawa and Delaware Indians painted for war.

"We need to follow them, Bobby."

From forest cover, the two can observe the natives walking their horses, with two American captives riding tied together, into Chief Turkey Foot's village.

Attaching their horses to a branch, E.J. and Bobby smear mud on their already grimy faces and begin crawling forward. Shaded from the midday sun by a huge woodland canopy, they smell burning logs and hear the Algonquin language being spoken.

From a safe distance away, the two new prisoners are seen being shoved into a shelter while a third captive is having his head shaved by a sobbing Ottawa squaw.

"Let's get out of here, Bobby. We need to report this to Flinn and maybe we can do something to help these captives."

E.J. and Bobby ride back staying off the main path and fortunately locate Captain Flinn before he has dispatched the gathered scouts again.

"Get everybody off this trail, Captain; there is a village up ahead!" declares an excited E.J.

From the cover of deep woods, the young men advise Captain Flinn of what they encountered.

"Boys, I feel we are obligated to save those three," pronounces Flinn to the forty.

Early that evening at Turkey Foot's Ottawa village, Indians eat and laugh, a fire around a pole is stoked by children, and an American is painted black by the same squaw that shaved him earlier.

Crawling nearby again is E.J., Bobby, their friend McClellan and two other scouts from Flinn's corp.

"You remember the plan?" E.J. whispers to his companions. Barely detecting the men nodding in the faint light he continues. "If things go awry, the camp from two nights ago is the rendezvous."

Okay, fix your bayonet and pick out the Injun you're going to take out if they don't run."

Ten minutes of anticipation goes by until commotion and a gunshot from the outskirts at the other side of the small Indian community is heard. The decoy from Flinn's detachment rouses the village warriors.

Creeping forward in anticipation of a path being created from the braves' departure, E.J. takes the lead.

"There they go. Let's get them."

As the five sprint into the village, two surprised squaws raising tomahawks and beginning to holler are bayoneted. The liberators hustle to the hostages' wigwam area, pulling out two white captives while E.J. grabs the painted American near the fire and uses a hunting knife to slice through his leather wrist binding.

"Come on," commands E.J. to the black-painted white.

"My Indian wife," responds the captive in a familiar voice.

"Forget about her, let's go!" coerces E.J. as a surprised Ottawan racing in from relieving himself in the woods is bayoneted by Bobby.

Having collected the prisoners, the scouts flee the village.

Glancing back from reacting to Indian musket shots, Bobby sees two of his companions go down. Turning to protect a following

McClellan, he raises his hunting musket and empties a ball into a Delaware warrior.

"Ey Yii ah!" screams the Lenape.

"Keep running, E.J.!" yells Bobby.

"Let's get our two friends, Mac, before the Injuns do!"

"E.J.?" the escaping painted American wonders aloud while dashing into the forest.

Bobby and McClellan return past the two hightailing captives to help their injured comrades laying amongst the chaos.

Mid-June at the Grand Glaize has hundreds of warriors eager to head south to meet Wayne's army.

"I tell you, Lasselle, the scouts coming back from GreeneVille indicate the Americans have 1700, while our numbers total 2000 warriors and 1500 British."

"Sounds like you have them outnumbered, Running Deer," says Lasselle, grabbing a new musket ramrod from behind his traders counter.

"As usual, I am worried for you, my husband," asserts a listening Morning Bird.

"We have great leaders, my wife," assures Running Deer in Algonquin. "With the British with us, it will be easier than Harmar's and St. Clair's victories put together. There will be plenty of horses and supplies that will be effortless to take from Wayne. "

"What else do you need, Running Deer?" asks Lasselle.

Answering for her husband, Morning Bird interjects, "He needs a touch of humility from his Manitou and protection from the Great Spirit."

With so many Indian nations involved, leadership issues emerge as the coalition heads southerly through the Great Black Swamp.

"I do not know who introduced the rum, but Buckongahelas's Delaware and some others are staying behind in the Grand Glaize," claims Little Turtle.

"Too much celebration at the war powwow," imparts Chief LeGris.

"I'm surprised you are not with them, LeGris."

"I was. I can just handle it better."

"Blue Jacket insists that we leave without them," informs Little Turtle, glancing at LeGris. "The first departing division of 1250 warriors has the Wyandot, Shawnees, Ottawa, Chippewa and our Miami."

"No British?" asks LeGris.

"A few but not what was promised."

Simon Girty is somewhere with us dressed like an Indian. Probably thinks he'll have a better chance surviving if he gets captured by the Americans."

"Ha! I don't think so," laughs LeGris. "Turtle, word is getting around that these Mackinac and Saginaw warriors that joined us just two days ago were late because they ravaged the women of warriors from the north who were already at the Glaize."

"I forgot they were among the coalition now. We will see how that plays out, LeGris. I am concerned about this Chief Bear of the northern Ottawa and some others. They are very aggressive, much like Blue Jacket."

Progress of the 1250 is slowed by the underestimated amount of food deemed necessary by the British. Hunting the plentiful deer and bear is required and necessitates stopping the progression at one or two o'clock in the afternoon. To accelerate the eagered encounter with the Americans, Chief Bear sends the newly arriving Mingo with the Wyandot to follow the discovered yellow-ribboned Choctaw and Chickasaw American spies toward Fort GreeneVille. The rest of the federation heads for Fort Recovery, stopping short to hunt and plan their strategy.

"Bear, if we are patient and focus only on the supply trains, we can starve these Americans to extinction," argues Little Turtle. "We have so many warriors, and more on the way, that no Americans will be able to travel safely outside their forts."

"The arrogant Wayne builds on top of the battlefield we were victorious at," rants Blue Jacket. "I say we do both. The British artillery soldiers with us only need the cannons we hid to knock down the walls of this Fort Recovery."

"Waiting for what our spies say is the only patience I will display, Little Turtle," claims Bear. "I do not like this tiny Fort Recovery either, Blue Jacket. Almost as much as I dislike some brothers in our alliance."

Inside Fort Recovery early in the morning of June 30, E.J. sits, gleeful and stunned.

"I can't believe what I'm seeing," says E.J., staring across the table at his Uncle Isaac. "Now that you have that bear grease off you, it's becoming more real."

"Ha, well it does keep mosquitoes off a person," comments Isaac, sipping coffee. "I'm just really sorry those two rangers had to die saving me."

"They would have done it for anybody, Ike," says Bobby, trying to comfort him. "No one was going to watch you or anyone else go up in flames."

"We still haven't seen the other two captives yet," comments E.J., then pausing. "You have to tell us again, Uncle Isaac, how you managed—"

Bam, bam.

Ike jumps and reacts. "Fellas, I have been hearing those shots all morning. Isn't anyone concerned?"

Captain Alexander Gibson, the fort commander finishing his breakfast nearby, speaks up. "We hear that every day, Mr. Carlisle. Relax. It is either our hunters or the Injuns that are seen occasionally roaming about."

"I saw where you sent out four troops to check the area, Captain. That's much appreciated," says Major William McMahon.

"Everything looks good for your convoy back to GreeneVille, Major," assures Captain Gibson.

"Tell the supply train to go ahead, Captain, will ya? I'll catch up with them as soon as I finish breakfast and hear the rest of this Ike's story," says McMahon, chewing his food and looking for a cup of coffee.

"Well," begins Isaac, "during that battle at Kekionga, I was with the cavalry in that charge we were making. As we closed in on those Indians with our swords out, heavy fire—from I don't know where for sure—struck the horse I was riding. The horse fell in such a manner that I ended up under him, knocking the wind out of me and pinning me. Unable to move, it was a good thing that horse and I fell into a briar thicket. The redskins could have easily finished me off. Through the gun smoke, haze and weeds, I could scarcely make out the battle. Oh, there was some horrible things going on."

"That's probably when I was down in the shallow riverbed, and Bobby saved my life," adds E.J. "Go on, Ike."

"It took a while to wiggle myself out from under that dead horse, and then I waited till nightfall to make sure it was safe to leave."

"Where did the Indians catch you?" asks Bobby.

"I was on my way back to Fort Washington for a few days after the battle, following the trail southeast the best I could remember, when out of nowhere, Delaware warriors appeared."

"How in the world did you survive almost three years?" asks E.J.

"I would bet, if I was a betting man, plenty of prayer," says the pastor, suddenly appearing.

"Prayed every morning, Pastor," says Ike, standing up to give him a greeting.

"God is not finished with you here on earth yet, Ike."

"By the way," remarks Uncle Isaac, "I haven't seen Ben yet. Is he out scouting? I figure he and you guys were inseparable."

Uproar and shouting clamors from the corner blockhouses facing the southerly trail.

"Injuns! Indian attack!" discloses a voice. "On the forest trail, the packhorse train is getting attacked!"

McMahon, running out the mess hall door from the breakfast table, grabs his musket.

"Come on, Hartshorne! Let's go, riflemen! Dang!" McMahon yells, sprinting out the south gate.

"There in the forest, Major!" informs a blockhouse guard pointing southerly.

"Hold up, men. Let's get our horses!" orders McMahon. "They're too far away."

Shots in St. Clair's trace forest trail are intense as McMahon, leading thirty dragoons, rides through a returning stampede of horses.

"YI, YI, YI!" yells Chief Bear, leading the follow-up butchery of packhorse drivers running back toward the safety of Fort Recovery.

"Cut them off!" commands a waving Little Turtle. "Don't let them get back! Grab the packhorses!"

Entering the forest portion of the trail, McMahon, leading with Kekionga veteran Captain Asa Hartshorne, is met by a force of Native Americans. He immediately is shot from his horse and is writhing on the ground.

"I know this American!" yells a scalping knife-carrying warrior. "I want his heart!" Ignoring the altercations around him, he pulls it out and consumes it.

Hartshorne, struck down as well, swings his sword at warriors and shouts, "You will not take me alive!"

Two natives dodge his long blade and tomahawk him to death.

Americans retreating back toward Fort Recovery are protected by gunfire from the garrison. Lieutenant Samuel Drake and Ensign Dold are permitted out of the gates with twenty men, including E.J., Bobby, Mac and a newly freed Uncle Isaac. The twenty cover the flanks with musket and pistol fire to hold off the ensuing warriors, and then help the wounded survivors in through the gate.

"Drake is hit, get him in here!" orders Gibson.

Bobby and E.J. run out and drag the lieutenant back in.

"Hold up! Surround the fort. But no closer! Pick them off from here!" commands Bear.

"Fire!" yells Blue Jacket to his Shawnee.

Like hailstones battering a wood roof, hundreds of musket balls from 1000 coalitionists slam against the fort walls.

"Chief Bear!" yells a British officer, pointing. "Order your Chippewa and Ottawa to attack that picket wall of the fort!"

"Ah yi Yi Yi!" scream a hundred natives, rushing the fifteen-foot-high fort curtain. Axes and tomahawks are frantically slammed into the picket fence to create a passage inside. Mysteriously, some Indians are struck in the back by musket balls and fall wounded or dead.

Guns pointed through the wall cracks by the garrison are ignited, killing and wounding more natives and forcing a retreat.

"Where are the cannons hidden?" asks British Captain Beaubien to Ottawa Chief Little Otter. After a brief search of the known hiding spots, none are found.

Discouraged, the natives and British gaze at the fort blockhouses just as loud booms from howitzers fill the air. The weapon hunters drop to the ground, listening to grapeshot pass overhead.

Inside Fort Recovery, musket balls hitting the walls of the fort can be heard. Groans from the thirty-six wounded Americans keep Surgeon Mate James Andrews moving from fractured elbows and arms to splintered knees.

"I think I know what Chief Underwood was trying to tell us this morning, Captain," says interpreter Donaldson.

"Oh yeah, what's that?" retorts a smirking Gibson.

"That there were a lot of Indians seen approaching."

"Oh, really? What was your first clue?" asks Gibson sarcastically, flinching as a musket ball, finding its way between picket logs, whizzes by.

"No really, I think I'm getting the hang of it.

"Chief Underwood!" calls Donaldson in the Muskogean language, "Over here. Tell the captain what you were telling me, only slower."

As the yellow-ribboned chief speaks, he animates and points outside the fort.

"Captain, he says his brothers have removed their yellow ribbons and are amongst the Injuns, blending in and shooting the enemy during attacks!"

From the tree-lined perimeter surrounding Fort Recovery, late afternoon closes with the British shaking their heads in dismay as the disorganized braves discharge lead balls into the fort walls with zero results.

"We need to meet and talk this over, Bear," suggests Little Turtle, with a British officer next to him.

"Let's move back, leave a few warriors here to keep an eye on the American fort while we powwow," replies the northern Ottawa designated leader.

Word is sent to all chiefs to assemble at the camp a half mile away.

Chippewa and Shawnee warriors who arrive at the powwow camp first shove each other and threaten death to one another.

"Hold up, Hold up! What is the problem?" asks Blue Jacket.

"Your braves fired upon us and the Ottawa when we attacked the fort!" screams a Chippewa. "I would say the Miami did too! And where are the Delaware?"

"We are not enemies. Why would that happen?" quizzes Blue Jacket.

"Hold up!" yells Bear, demanding silence. "Each of you tribal chiefs, take your braves to your camp and report back. No food until we decide our strategy."

"I count twenty American prisoners in our hands from the earliest attack," says Little Turtle. "Let's get some information, Bear."

Late in the day, from the southeast-corner two-story blockhouse, Fort Recovery commander Gibson and Ensign Dold peer down the St. Clair trace.

"Except for sporadic shots, most of the Indians have disappeared into the forest. What do you think of that, Ensign?

"If you are thinking of going out there, I wouldn't go yet, Captain. You may want to wait till tomorrow morning."

"You're probably right. They could be planning their next move."

"They may think they gave us a good licking, but I count seventeen dead Injuns at the gate alone and some more where they tried to hack a hole in the wall."

"We have at least twenty missing, judging by our dead lying out there and what we have in the fort," says Gibson. "Hate losing Major McMahon. He was a heck of a scout and Injun fighter."

"Yes, I liked him, too. How many natives and I saw some British too, do you think they have?"

"Has to be over 500. We had 140 troops protecting the convoy, and they were overwhelmed. I have to admit, I didn't see that coming. It had been calm around here for several months."

At midnight in Fort Recovery, many in the fort are resting or asleep while the Indian coalition prepares for an attack.

"We had great success this morning, taking over 300 horses and killing many whites," exclaims Little Turtle. "We have them right where we want them."

"You are too cautious, Turtle," complains Bear. "Under the cover of dark and now fog, our braves can move in undetected and take back our victory grounds."

You think that is such a good idea? Your Ottawa and the Chippewa, Saginaw and Mackinac should attack first," says Little Turtle. "The Miami will have no part of that plan."

"Let's let the Saginaw and Mackinac initiate the attack," suggests Bear. "We'll give them the first shot at coalition glory!"

"This way, my friends," directs Simon Girty, leading hundreds of Native Americans by torchlight back to encircle Fort Recovery. "By daybreak, this fortress will be in flames, and every American scalp from inside will be hanging from our waists!"

Stopping short of the open ground before the fort, coalitionists are unaware of the American-friendly Chickasaw and Chocktaw Indians that are spaced out behind them.

Crawling closer with hatchets, axes and tomahawks, the two northernmost Indian tribes' warriors are about to begin a third coalition assault.

Sleep is hard to get inside Fort Recovery because of the constant moaning of wounded Americans.

Peeking in the commander's office, Ensign Dold spies Gibson writing by candlelight. "Get some sleep, Captain. Natives don't usually attack at night," he says. "I'll keep watch for a while."

"I'm just putting finishing touches on this report, Ensign. What did we have, over 30 head of cattle taken?"

"INDIANS!" comes a cry from the northeast corner blockhouse.

Gibson, Dold and the able 250 Americans man the blockhouses and climb the banquette to fire over the fifteen-foot-high picket wall.

"They're below us!" expresses an American from atop the barrier.

"They are trying to hack their way in again!"

Glimpses of the 200 warriors can be seen from the blockhouse, and muskets are cross-fired from the embrasures into the warriors, with lethal results.

"They're climbing up ropes and ladders!" alerts Gibson. "You six riflemen, go to the southeast blockhouse to pour more musket fire into them, and see if the howitzer can't be directed to fire along the wall!"

"E.J.! Jam your bayonet between the pickets!" orders Bobby. "The redskins are leaning against the wall to chop!"

"Okay, Bobby!"

"Ayiiii yaya!" is heard from the outside as a blade pierces a Saginaw.

"Bobby, if you're loaded, fire through this small slot they've opened up!" yells E.J. while jamming his ramrod into the barrel of his Charleville.

BAM!

More screams come from outside the palisade.

Flaming arrows flying overhead light up the fort curtain enough to see warriors falling backward from ladders and down from ropes.

"They're shooting their own," mutters Gibson to himself. Peering out the narrow blockhouse window, he sees musket flashes from the Indian perimeter. "Keep firing, boys!"

Warriors outside the palisade assist in carrying their brothers away to the safety of darkness.

"Put out those fires, men!" orders Ensign Dold.

"It's a miracle, Pastor!" calls E.J. from atop the east barrier to the clergyman assisting an injured soldier. "They're retreating!"

Chapter 13

July 1794 — Fort GreeneVille and on the trail to the Grand Glaize

"General! I have news for you," states Lieutenant Harrison through the headquarters door. "You need to hear this!"

"Another dispute settled by a duel, Harrison?" Wayne suggests from his bed. "These so-called gentlemen need to settle their differences in a better way. Come in, Lieutenant."

Stepping through the entryway, Harrison leads Corporal Thompson and Private Hunter into the office/living quarters of Anthony Wayne.

"These men just rode in, sir. The sounds heard last night by blockhouse guards confirm these men's story!"

"What's that, Lieutenant?"

"Fort Recovery has been under siege for two days. These two left under the cover of musket fire to get here. Captain Gibson needs help!"

"That's right, General. Fort Recovery is surrounded by hundreds of warriors. I still don't know how Private Hunter and I made it through the Indians to get here.

"I don't disagree; I see a couple musket holes in your hats. Tell me more." comments Wayne now sitting on the edge of his bed.

"General, Captain Gibson reports he needs troops, food and medical supplies," renders Thompson.

"I knew this could happen, but I thought our scouts would warn us."

"Maybe they were killed before they could, sir," suggests Harrison.

"Let's see, Harrison. It's 1 p.m. I want Captain Brock to prepare to take two companies of dragoons and our Choctaw friends with the supplies the corporal requested plus ammunition and artillery rounds."

"Yes sir."

"Have them take some cattle. All this leaves in the morning. Get started, Harrison. DeButts, I need you in here."

"Yes sir."

"The dragoons have returned, but we are waiting on General Scott and Todd's militia, correct?"

"Dragoons have returned from Kentucky, sir. They escorted in a supply train yesterday. The militia from Kentucky shall be escorting supplies and cattle, as well. I have not heard when they will arrive."

"We need to move this along faster. This legion needs to be prepared to march north in two weeks!"

"Yes sir."

"What about you two, Thompson, Hunter? Bet you're tired," asks Wayne.

"All we need are fresh horses," replies Corporal Thompson, "and then we'll be heading back to Fort Recovery, General."

Two days later, the tardy Delaware Chief Buckongahelas leading 500 warriors exits the Great Black Swamp, where he eyes Bear and a large portion of the battered Native American confederation heading north.

"Bear," calls Buckongahelas. "Bear Chief!"

Ignoring the greeting at first, Bear pulls the reins of his horse over to allow the procession to continue by.

Signaling Chief Pipe to take the Lenape forward, Buckongahelas turns to Bear and says, "I am bringing reinforcements."

"Does it look like we are happy to see you?" asks Bear, watching wounded being helped.

"You have many warriors, Bear. Let the wounded go back to the Grand Glaize while you join us in destroying Wayne."

"We have done our part, Buckongahelas. We have traveled many miles to help your cause. It is time for us to go home."

"Where are the British? Are Little Turtle and Blue Jacket still there?"

Just then, a horse-drawn litter, led by redcoats, passes by proceeding north.

Chief Buckongahelas recognizes the passenger, sprawled and jarring about, and calls, "Captain Beaubien, we have a shaman and magic powers for you."

"It is too late," responds a British officer leading the bier.

"What did he say?" asks Buckongahelas.

"He is dead," answers Chief Bear as he yanks the reins of his horse to follow the redcoat.

300 yards away at the edge of a meadow—hidden by large oak, cottonwood, hickory and walnut trees—are American spies Christopher Miller and the ever active Ensign Dold.

Watching the procession of warriors and British travel by, they pick up key information.

"I have taken their route before, Dold."

"Does it take them to the Glaize?"

"Yes. The trail we crossed a half hour ago would take you northwest to Kekionga."

At Fort GreeneVille, almost a month has gone by before General Anthony Wayne's army is fully ready to debouch.

"Major Buell, the legion is moving out July 28. You're in charge at GreeneVille while I'm gone," says Wayne. "There are 520 troops and thirty Choctaws at your disposal. Use them wisely."

"Yes sir."

"Keep pressing the seven Indian prisoners for information. In fact, the Choctaw should be good for bringing more captives in."

Keep the supplies moving forward, as well as information. You understand, Buell?" asks Wayne, sitting down in a sweat from a gout attack. "You have 700 Kentuckians to protect the convoys."

"You've told me that before, sir."

"Well, I'm telling you that again, dag nabbit! Don't you address me like that, or I'll demote you on the spot!"

Pausing, Wayne continues. "My will is in the top drawer, Buell. See that my son Isaac and daughter Margretta receive the letter if anything happens to me."

"Yes, General."

"That goes for all the other wills the men have turned in, Major."

Late afternoon of July 29 at Fort Recovery, E.J. is one of the fort occupants receiving a letter from a horseback advance guard of General Wayne's legion.

"It's from Charlotte, Pastor. It says they will not allow her to travel with the legion since she is pregnant. Especially since she lost the first baby."

"Babies and kids crying is not a good idea, "says the pastor, peering over the wall at trailblazers widening the path north.

"Is that a joke, Pastor?" asks Bobby, overhearing the conversation.

"Cause Wayne's band can be heard a couple miles away."

"Ha! As you know, Bobby, it's supposed to keep the army moving at a steady pace."

"Alright, you boys ready to join the United States legion?" asks Uncle Isaac, pulling his horse by the reins past the conversationists.

"Ike, E.J. and I are waiting for reassignment since Flinn's service expired and he went home," says Bobby. "Are you sure you want to rejoin after the last two and a half years?"

Uncle Isaac stops, turns around and asks, "Now, where am I going to go? I'd say over half the men in this army have lost kin to the redskins and are out for payback."

"Yeah, I see what you mean," replies Bobby.

"Captain Gibson and his riflemen are assembling outside the fort already," informs E.J., stepping down from the banquette.

"The legion can't be going too much farther this late in the day," says Bobby, leading his horse toward the gate.

Uncle Isaac gives out a whistle from the south fort gate and shouts, "Captain Gibson wants everyone assembled outside! Even those that will remain at Fort Recovery!"

Outside the east wall, the men joining the legion are told their departure is being delayed.

"Tie your horses up, boys, let's see what they want," orders Captain Gibson. "Line up, men!" yells Gibson at the 250 survivors of the siege.

Walking wounded, on makeshift crutches and tree-limb canes, make their way out the fort gates assisted by soldier friends.

The band leading Wayne's legion stops 100 yards away and plays marching music.

Hundreds of members of the legion's left wing, escorting the wagons, cannons, packhorses and cattle, stop temporarily and cheer.

"Hip hip hooray! Hip hip hooray! Hip hip hooray!" is heard by the fort defenders as they watch hats being waved.

Major General Anthony Wayne, accompanied by his aide-de-camps, gallops up to the aligned fort occupants. Halting his horse and scanning from left to right at the double straight line, Wayne turns and signals for the band to stop playing. From the top of his horse he shouts, "You are the bravest boys in the world!"

Dismounting, Wayne walks up to Gibson and pats him on the shoulder. Then Wayne proceeds speechlessly, slowly walking, inspecting, and patting each soldier on the shoulder. When he greets the wounded and sights seventeen graves, he is unable to hold the tears back.

That night, Little Turtle, Blue Jacket and Buckongahelas and 600 warriors lurk about the forests, probing for weaknesses in Wayne's 2500-man legion and militia.

"You can try to unnerve him all you want, Blue Jacket," offers Little Turtle, "but as we saw last fall, the black snake does not sleep."

"You give this Wayne too much credit, Turtle. Every one of these American generals has their flaw."

"Where do you think this American army is heading?" asks Buckongahelas.

"Same place Harmar and St. Clair were—Kekionga," answers Blue Jacket.

"Yes, Kekionga," responds Buckongahelas. "Richardville and your sister Tah Cum Wah are still there, are they not, Little Turtle?"

"Last I heard, they were," answers Turtle.

"Yes, that is where they must be heading," expresses Blue Jacket.

"Jacket, the confederation campaign has too many shortcomings," says a dejected Little Turtle. "When wisdom is replaced by emotion, my services are no longer needed," concludes Little Turtle.

Two days later, a few miles ahead of a bogged-down legion, American scouts and advance guards proceed.

"That Ephraim Kibbey and his forty sure know their way around," comments Bobby, surveying the swamp forest trail that the veteran frontiersman from Cincinnati disappears into.

"We may not see them for a while," says E.J. "I heard they are heading to a place called the Glaize on the other side of the swamp."

"I don't know how far that is, but I noticed that trail surveyor Newman wanted to turn left back there at the Kekionga trail."

"Ha! I didn't see that."

"Major Price had to inform him we are cutting through the swamp heading slightly northeast. He acted surprised."

A few miles back, the legion's right flank movement is slow.

"I tell you, this Wayne's got to be the biggest fool there is having us build a bridge in the middle of a swamp," grumbles Captain Guion, swatting mosquitoes away.

"You'd think we could have found a way around this quagmire," complains Major Cushing, checking his pocket watch, "but no, Wayne's stubbornness keeps us here ten hours."

"The best thing about this delay is watching that 'dandy' get his uniform a little muddy riding by inspecting his fancy bridge. Dang fool."

"Our only hope of success on this mission is Wayne getting sick or something and General Wilkinson taking over."

The next day, the main force reaches the St. Marys River, and the usual camp breastworks and accommodations are established.

"Captain Wells."

"Yes, General?"

"This will be a good place to rest and to build a supply storage fort. Besides that, according to the surgeon, swamp fever, malaria or something is affecting me and the men."

"Yes, it can be rough on a person if you're not use to this place, General," sympathizes William Wells. "I just want to tell you the river here flows westerly and then north to Kekionga."

"That's nice to know, Wells.

"Major Burbeck! Major Burbeck, get over here!"

"Yes, General," says the fort-building engineer, walking up from watching men catch salmon and trout.

"Build us a post across the river with two blockhouses."

"You want the men to cut the trees on this side of the river and assemble the fort over there?" questions Burbeck.

"Yes, and get started now!" shouts Wayne.

"I've seen the water waist-high over there, General," interjects William Wells.

"That's where it's going to be built, Wells! You got that?" emphasizes Wayne. "And I want Major Price's advance guard to get a little exercise. Have them cut the trees!

"Wells, I have an assignment for you and Kibbey." Looking around, he suddenly questions, "Geez, who's out there guarding us? Lieutenant Harrison, get a company protecting our perimeter."

"Yes sir."

"Alright Wells, take your favorite scouts and head for this place called the Glaize. See what's going on. Captain Kibbey, take your forty westerly, see if the Wabash Indians are up to anything, and check out Kekionga.

"I want you back here in four days."

At the Grand Glaize on the banks of the Auglaize and Maumee Rivers, the village leadership listens to a visitor.

"Who do you say you are?" asks Ottawa Chief Little Otter staring at the white man.

Acting as an interpreter, British trader John Kinzie relays the conversation. "He says his name is Newman, Robert Newman."

"What do you want, Newman? And it better be good, because that white flag you have isn't worth much right now," says Kinzie.

"I am from Wayne's army."

"Let me take his scalp right now," steps in Running Deer, understanding English.

Placing a hand on Running Deer's chest, Kinzie attempts to calm the young warrior. "Take it easy, let's hear what he has to say first."

"Wayne's legion is coming here. Not Kekionga."

Back in Philadelphia, congressmen and administration sort through some mail.

"This guy writes that General Wayne is drunk all the time, lying around in his headquarters," says Thomas Jefferson.

"Who signed it?" asks Secretary of War Knox.

"It's anonymous."

"That's typical," responds President Washington. "The other day I had one, oh, here it is," showing James Madison, "complaining about how incompetent Wayne was and that he hangs anyone who disagrees with him. Did I detect a Spanish word in that letter?" questions Washington.

"Hmmm, yes there is. That's interesting," notes Madison.

"I say we leave the man alone. The last message we received from him was that a fort he had built held off an attack by Little Turtle," reveals Secretary Knox.

Thwack, Thwack, Thwack, Thwack, Thwack!

"Timber!" yells E.J. as another ash tree destined for the new fort crashes near the St. Marys River, startling a familiar face.

"What are you doing in that water?" hollers Bobby. "Fishing with your bare hands?"

"Dad burnit! Can't a man have a little privacy while he bathes? Ha!" laughs a skinny-dipping Private John Smith.

"You better watch it, Smitty! The pioneers are moving this way to cut more down," informs E.J.

Ignoring the chopping near the river and the legion tents, Smith asks, "There's no women around, is there, fellas?"

"Here's your clothes, Smitty," discloses a grinning Bobby, handing him his belongings.

"Gracias, senior," says Smith.

"What the heck? Are you speaking Spanish?"

"Oh, it's that General Wilkinson I've been assigned to. Some of the mailings are handed off to Spaniards. Whoa, whoa, what the heck?!" yells Smitty. "Did you see that beech tree fall into General Wayne's tent?"

The next day, early in the morning at newly christened Fort Adams, the legion departs.

"Can you believe it? I'm left with fifty men in the middle of hostile territory," laments Lieutenant James Underhill, watching the last wagons of Wayne's legion disappear into the Black Swamp.

"I wouldn't have done this to you, Lieutenant," sympathizes General James Wilkinson, looking down from his horse.

"If Wayne hadn't survived that tree falling on him, you'd be the one leading us north, General," declares Lieutenant William Clark saddled next to him.

"At least we wouldn't be moving out today, Lieutenant," says Wilkinson. "We wouldn't be leaving Underhill here with the sick, the invalids and an unfinished fort, either. My God, the blockhouses don't even have roofs on them, let alone, a gate to this post."

"Did you see 'His Excellency' riding around here yesterday like a peacock, showing everyone he had survived?" expresses Clark. "Who does he think he is, God?"

Observing the rear guards following up and anxious to get going, Wilkinson concludes, "The good thing is, the scouts have not spotted any large amounts of natives around, Lieutenant."

"That doesn't mean they can't come later," claims a dispirited Underhill.

A few miles onto the swamp trail in a watery, thick-forested section, Wayne, ahead of the band, sights aide-de-camp Harrison riding in from the advance guard.

"We are missing a surveyor, sir. Robert Newman's been gone a couple days. His horse is gone, also."

"I'd guess Injuns got him, Harrison," offers Wayne, swiping gnats and mosquitoes away from his face.

"Could be, sir," offers Harrison, riding alongside the General. "I noticed he did like working alone. Trouble is, he is far too experienced to let that happen to him."

"You think he's deserted, don't you, Lieutenant?"

"I'd say if we locate him at the Glaize, he will have a lot of questions to answer, General."

"Lieutenant, find Wells and Kibbey. Inform them to take their units ahead to screen the main force."

Thirty miles up the swamp trail at the Grand Glaize, preparations are being made to evacuate.

"Not again, Running Deer," speaks Morning Bird. "Is this not Kekionga all over again?"

"I don't like it, either. But you and our baby in your womb need to leave."

"What about you?" asks Morning Bird in Algonquin.

"I prefer to take a stand here against the white devils invading our land."

"You know, Little Turtle advocates making peace with the Americans, Running Deer. Why do we not follow his leadership?"

"McKee and Girty assure me that stopping this American invasion means the whites will leave us alone forever."

"At what price? I do not want to lose my husband, father of our child and clan over land. Can we not hunt and farm among these whites in peace?"

"The British wisdom inform us that that will never happen. The hatred between whites and natives is too great.

"I am sorry, my wife. Our people need to move to the rapids and combine our warriors with the British."

Chapter 14

August 8 – 20, 1794 — The Grand Glaize, Roche de Bout, Fallen Timbers (Present-day Defiance and Maumee, Ohio)

Standing at the southwest point formed by the Auglaize and Maumee Rivers, Wayne sees smoke from smoldering cabins and wigwams that had been torched, the aftermath of vacated Native Americans.

"You called for me, General Wayne?" asks the pastor.

"I'm waiting on Reverend David Jones to show any day now, but I'm glad you are with us, Pastor," remarks Wayne. "I know you have seen war before. I just want to voice my appreciation for your service and prayers."

"It's God's calling that I'm here."

"We came out of the swamp with many soldiers with fever and shakes. My gout is acting up, and my leg the tree fell on is nearly broken. We need some divine intervention, Pastor," expresses a limping Wayne, glancing at the river current flowing northeasterly.

"General, the Lord has a purpose for everything and everyone. Every battle you were in during the war, God could have called you home. Every close call, including a near miss by a falling tree, was divine intervention from God to put you in this position at this place in time."

"You think so, Pastor? Well, we need some more."

"Each person is given a talent by God at birth. Yours is to lead this legion you have been preparing and marching, to whatever the Lord has in store for it."

"Why was there no battle here, Pastor? Why was it so easy taking this huge village?"

"God's ways are not like ours, General. The next encounter may be a challenge. Even King David had his struggles."

"Amen, Pastor," concludes Wayne turning away, eyes searching for Major Henry Burbeck. "Build it here, Burbeck! Right here on this point!"

"Are you sure, General? That plot across the Maumee facing here is better land," suggests Burbeck.

"What did I just say, Major? I want it built here with four blockhouses, one at each corner just like Fort Recovery. I want it so strong that we will defy any enemy from taking it!"

Thirty-eight miles northeast at the Roche de Bout, American-friendly Choctaw and Chickasaw blend in among the 3000 occupants. For six white spies, it is a challenge.

"None of you can speak Algonquin or Odawa?" questions the painted, topless William Wells.

"A phrase here or there," answers Robert McClellan.

"Pull your feathers down a bit. Dang. It looks like you smeared your paint, Mac," declares the head American spy.

"We're all a little nervous about this," admits Paschall Hickman.

"I can understand that. The rest of you look authentic. We're going to ride into Roche de Bout real slow. Like we know what we're doing.

"Just let me do the talking."

A half hour later, the six ease into a community of wigwams, cabins and campfires that includes twelve different tribes intermingled with French and British.

After spending the day visiting with unsuspecting natives, two isolated Shawnee warriors near British Fort Miami are lured away.

"How many British are in the fort?" asks Wells.

"I do not know," answers the Shawnee.

"I think you both know a lot. Just don't yell out," whispers a calm Wells, brandishing a scalping knife while the two are surrounded.

"I know your people are short on food. We have plenty where we come from," bribes a lying Wells. "All you have to do is cooperate, and you can keep your scalp, too."

"200 British."

"Warriors?"

"700 with 500 on the way."

"How did you know the legion was coming to the Glaize?"

"An American named Newman told us."

The other Shawnee speaks up, "Newman and Alexander McKee are at Detroit recruiting militia."

While skirting around the village and heading back to Fort Defiance with their two prisoners that evening, William Wells notices a bright marquee from the 1791 Wabash battle.

"Let's see if there is more information inside," expresses Wells.

"Don't press it, Wells," asserts McClellan. "Let's go home."

"As before, just let me do the talking."

Leaving two to guard the Shawnees and horses, four enter the tent. Surprised it contains fifteen Delaware around a campfire, the spies squeeze in and sit cross-legged.

"We bring you friendship," greets Wells in Algonquin, observing quizzical nods in return.

"Who are you?" asks a chief, glancing at McClellan curiously.

"Eel River Miami," orates Wells. "We are passing through to fight Americans."

"What is your name?" asks another Delaware.

"Golden Eagle," answers Wells. "This is Setting Sun, and the—" pointing at McClellan.

"No, let him speak," requests an older brave staring at McClellan.

"You speak!" demands a now glaring brave, pointing at Mac.

Unnerved and not waiting for Wells, McClellan blurts out, "Blue Bird," in English.

"I know what Miami look like," conveys the wild-eyed older brave.

"No Miami! Me'liken. These are Americans!"

Wells pulls a pistol from his leggings.

BAM!

Discharging his firearm into the chief, Wells shouts, "Get out of here!"

Bam, bam, bam.

The other three Americans fire their hidden pistols into the nearest warrior as they scramble to exit the tent to their horses.

"Let's go! Let's go! Let's go!" urges McClellan, running and leaping spread eagle over the back quarter of his saddleless mount, landing atop.

The six spies and two cooperating Shawnee grab their reins and give side kicks to their mares to bolt away.

Musket balls and knives from the Delaware whiz by the fleeing intelligencers, except for two. Wells and McClellan are hit.

The next day at the Grand Glaize, fort construction is too slow for General Wayne.

"Give these Kentuckians some axes. How many extra do we have?"

"One hundred forty, sir," answers aide-de-camp DeButts.

"Then pass them out to 'em. Speed this up! Maybe some hard work will relieve some of the disrespect they have. Let me see that punishment report again, DeButts!"

"Here you go, sir."

"Twenty-five lashes for cussing out General Scott. Twenty-five for refusal of a guard duty order. Twenty-five lashes for falling asleep on guard duty. You know, DeButts, let's rethink this. I'm reconsidering these court martial decrees. The volunteers provide some great fighters. They are giving their time and being paid very little. Let them out of the guard house and put them to work. I want to pardon these sentences. But let it be known, this is a warning!"

Two days later at the Roche de Bout in the middle of the Maumee River, Native Americans powwow.

"The whites have dug in on the southwest point of the Glaize, Turkey Foot," says Little Turtle. "It will take British cannons and military to help us stop this American force and then uproot the fort they've established."

"Yes, it is not going to be without bloodshed."

"I urge peace. Take advantage of this last offering of peace we received yesterday from this General Wayne."

"No! We should never trust the white devil," interjects Blue Jacket. "We can never give in to this threat to our way of life and the taking of our land!"

"I am sorry, Little Turtle. I have to agree with Blue Jacket," responds Ohio Ottawa Chief Turkey Foot. "Did we not come to your aide at Kekionga four years ago and at the Wabash three years ago to destroy these invaders?"

"The Wyandotte are with you, Turkey Foot," conveys Chief Tarhe. "The British are standing with us with the strong fort they built not far from here."

"No disrespect, Tarhe, but where is the food the British promised?" asks Little Turtle. "Our people are starving. Where were the cannons against the Wabash River fort? Why does it always take Simon Girty and Alexander McKee to convince you the British will help us?"

"This is it, Turtle," speaks Shawnee war Chief Black Hoof. "They have to help us. Our backs are literally against the Great Lake Erie. Our people must fight to the end!"

At the American fort at the Glaize the next day, the legion awaits the order to advance farther northeast.

"General, you've been in bed for five days, your gout is flaring and your knee is infected!" informs the surgeon.

"Dad burnit! I know I've been in bed. It's time to move out! So get me to my horse and help me on! I can't let my legion see me like this!"

"General, do you remember Wells's report?" asks aide-de-camp Lewis, assisting Wayne out of his tent.

"Yes I do, and how is he and McClellan doing?"

"They won't be with us for a while, sir," reveals Lewis. "They are in the infirmary building with wounds to the wrist and shoulder blade, respectively."

"I know that. I didn't ask that, dad burnit! We're going to miss them. Is Kibbey out there?"

"Kibbey and his scouts are reconning the route, sir, and will be leading the way."

"I need to see Major Hunt," remarks Wayne while Lewis, the surgeon and William Henry Harrison boost him into his saddle.

"Here he comes, General," conveys Harrison, observing Thomas Hunt exiting the fort.

"General, you look good up there," declares the new fort commander.

"Don't bull-crap me, Major! I feel bad and I look bad. Now, did you come up with a name for this stockade?"

"You gave us the inspiration for it, General. It is Fort Defiance, if that is okay with you."

"I like it, and Major, I have known you well for a long time. You are well qualified to defend it with every expense of blood."

Returning a salute, Wayne turns his horse to leave with his aides-de camp on either side of him. Riding down the river embankment and across a shallow ford to the north side of the Maumee, he sees the already assembled legion and Kentucky militia awaiting their commander.

"Sir, General Wilkinson and the 1st Sub-legion will follow the south bank parallel to us for a few miles," advises Lieutenant Harrison.

"You think of that all by yourself, Harrison?"

"No, you did, General. You didn't feel well, but that was an order, sir."

"Very good. I was ready to give you credit! Ha! Start up the band!"

Three unimpeded days later, the legion enters another large vacated Indian village.

"Ah, the infamous Roche de Bout," conveys Wayne to the aides-de-camp. "Rock in the river, and there it is," pointing to the half-acre limestone outcrop the natives have been using for meetings.

"Let's halt here," asserts Wayne. "Harrison, this is where we miss William Wells."

"Yes sir."

"Send George Shrim and his scouts ahead of Kibbey's, and tell him to find the Indians. Kibbey's men will protect the perimeter of the legion and the volunteers behind us while—Burbeck! Major Burbeck, over here!"

"Yes sir, General."

"Go on, Harrison, get the scouts where they need to be.

"Burbeck, we need a temporary storage fort built here. When we go into battle, our troops need to be light and mobile."

"DeButts, find Captain Pike. He will be assigned 200 men to protect our supplies and belongings in this fort. Let's call it Fort Deposit. Pike needs to have twelve men standing guard around Fort Deposit at all times."

"Yes sir," replies DeButts, checking his list. "Pike is with the 1st Sub-legion. Anything else, sir?"

"The legion will be camping here to prepare for advancement into possible fighting. General order is still half rations for everyone until we get back to Fort Defiance."

Three miles downriver, a contingent of 1200 warriors, Canadian militia and British combatants strung out six deep for a mile wait for Wayne's legion to enter a meadow.

"When the Americans enter, Turkey Foot, encircle your Ottawa to the left near the ridge," orders Blue Jacket. "Tarhe and his Wyandotte will circle to the right."

Spotting Shrim's spies approaching a half mile away in tall grass, Blue Jacket reacts, "What is this? A few spies they send forth, or the army they lead?

"Slip down below the cliffs and circle them, Running Deer," commands Blue Jacket. "Let's probe this group and see what news they can give us."

Fifteen minutes later, no following army is detected, and Running Deer's mounted braves swoop in and corral Captain Shrim and his five scouts. Turning their horses to escape the trap, each of the Americans avoids fired musket balls and arrows, except for a formerly captured and released William May. Trailing the other five, May is caught and intentionally knocked off his ride.

Brought before Turkey Foot and Blue Jacket, he is questioned, and through Alexander McKee's English interpretation, May offers information.

"I'd say a total force of 500."

"This white has been caught before and has been proven untrustworthy," scoffs Blue Jacket. "Take him behind our line for target practice."

The next day, back at the nearly completed Fort Deposit, Captain Shrim reports to Wayne.

"The boys are still out there watching, General, but I wanted to tell you firsthand that we saw a glimpse of hundreds of redskins waiting for you to cross a meadow north of here about three miles. We lost a man, and I'm not sure how much information he has given up."

"Dad burnit, Captain. I'm going to send Major Price and his mounted scouts that way today to keep the rascals anxious."

"I'll tell ya somethin' else, General. They more than likely have been fasting. They like fighting on an empty stomach."

"Think they're getting hungry, Captain?"

"I know I am!"

"Okay, grab a bite and get back out there, dag nabbit!" orders Wayne.

"Harrison, the advancement begins tomorrow morning. Prime the men. The officers will meet tonight at my tent at seven for final instructions!"

"The braves did not encounter Wayne's army?" asks Buckongahelas to the council of chiefs gathered. "Where is Wayne? What are the Americans waiting on?"

"I do not know that, but their scouts that got away have surely told the black snake of our position," opines Blue Jacket.

"Let's move our line back to the tangled trees," suggests Turkey Foot. "It will be two miles from the British fort and provide better cover."

"I'll send a messenger to Tarhe of the plan," says Blue Jacket. "Meanwhile, it has been two days since we have eaten. If it is okay with our Kitchi Manitou, if nothing happens tonight, we should eat in the morning to regain some strength."

"I feel the Great Spirit approving that," declares Shawnee Chief Black Hoof.

"Running Deer, over here," calls Blue Jacket. "You have been surveilling all day. What have you seen?" "My spies encounter American scouts whenever we get close. There have been small skirmishes. I could not get a good count of the enemy's main force."

"The confederation appreciates you and your Miami staying with us."

"My brothers and I will be between the Shawnee and Delaware, Blue Jacket, at the center of the attack."

The next morning, thunderstorms over Fort Deposit have moved east of the Maumee.

"Alright, form it up, gentlemen," orders Wayne. "Kibbey, take your forty to the south side of the river, and make sure no redskins cross the river and get behind us."

"Okay, Gen'ral."

Gazing across the 600-yard-wide shallow Maumee River, aide-de-camp Lewis declares, "It's going to be a hot and steamy one today."
"It's going to be an even hotter one if you don't help me get up on this horse, dad burnit, Lewis!"

While being hoisted onto his black stallion, the general barks, "Everyone should have fixed bayonets, two days rations and a blanket, Harrison! Everyone's knapsacks should be in Fort Deposit!"

"Yes sir, those orders have been followed. In addition, Hamtramck's 4th Sub-legion, wearing green, is on the left ready to cut through the forest, sir. Wilkinson's 1st, wearing white, is on the right and will move along the ridge overlooking the flood plain."

"Alright, as in the plan, bring Major Burbeck's artillery and ammunition forward between Captain Kingsbury's 3rd, in yellow, and the 4th," orders Wayne.

"Yes sir, I'll see to that now," obeys Harrison.

"Lewis!" voices General Wayne, looking to the rear of the army of 2500. "See that the 2nd Sub-legion, in red, is positioned behind the 4th. We'll move them where we need them once we are engaged with the enemy."

Lewis salutes and rides to the rear guard area to follow orders.

"Did I hear the drums got wet? For crying out loud, DeButts!" complains General Wayne. "Have the drummers strike the drum rim to pace us."

Glancing around, Wayne—in his element—smiles with satisfaction and orders, "Sound the horns to move us out, DeButts. Maybe the drums will dry out by the time we encounter the rascals!"

Two hours into the march, Major Price's horseback advance scouts, spread out a half mile ahead of the legion, trek northeast. All eyes scan for movement as the scouts cross a meadow, then through a forest and another meadow.

"Awfully quiet out here, E.J.," comments Bobby, paired with his buddy again.

With his hunting musket across his lap atop his horse, E.J. answers softly, "If we start hearing bird calls all of a sudden, just be aware. Keep an eye on the vedettes ahead."

"I wouldn't want to be them, today. By the way, where's Ike assigned?"

"He's with the 4th's dragoons. Now dad burnit, stay al—"

Bam! Bam! Bam! Bam, BAM!

Discharged British Brown Bessie musket balls quickly take down the two vedettes as well as three fellow outriders.

"Dang!" E.J. spots one of the vanguards thirty yards away gathering to his feet. "Come on, Bobby, let's get this guy outta here."

"Heeya, giddy!" yells Bobby, prompting his horse.

"Injuns are comin' out after him, Bobby!"

Bam!

Bobby Fulton's pistol ignites, forcing the natives to drop to the ground.

E.J. scoops up the horseless American, and with Bobby by his side, they spur their steeds away from immediate danger toward the advance guard of the 3rd Sub-legion.

"No retreating! No retreating!" bellows an unfamiliar captain.

Bam. Bam.

"Geez, that's the yellow caps advancing. Let's get off and join them!" suggests a frantic Bobby.

"Get off and load up, buddy!" yells E.J., swatting his horse away.

Rapidly loading their modified Charleville rifles in the tall grass, the three can hear musket lead whizzing by and the Ottawa closing in.

Popping up and firing, the three scouts make little impact on a massive Ottawa charge and join the now-retreating advance guard.

Two companies of light infantry from Wilkinson's right wing stop the American retreat and slow the Potawatomie that are joining the Ottawa.

Anthony Wayne, surrounded by his aides-de-camp, is immediately aware of engagement as he hears numerous gun shots in the distance.

"Form the double lines and move forward," orders Wayne to DeButts and Lewis. Each ride off to carry the orders to sub-legion commanders.

A horseback courier bolts up to Wayne. "General, there is an Indian push at the front on the right!"

Suspected by Wayne, coalitionists are threatening the advance guard at all fronts.

"Burbeck, bring your howitzers up and point them toward the clearing on the right and the ridge of the flood plain. Do you see the issue?"

"I see it, sir!"

"Let's go then! Quickly! Set it up, 300 yards, canister shot! Fire when you're ready! We need to help the light infantry out till we get our dragoons and infantry into position to charge!"

BOOM! BOOM!

Six-pound howitzers pour iron canister fragments into a tall grass meadow of Indians and into the thick flood plain brush to prevent Wilkinson's 1st Sub-legion from being outflanked and overrun.

At the battle front, on the right, uncertainty prevails.

"Move back, Bobby, there are too many redskins!"

"I'll cover you as you load up."

Bam!

Bobby fires a second shot, this time from his pistol, temporarily slowing the Indian charge.

"Fall back, men, and to the right. We are going to flank them!" yells Captain Cooke.

Six-pounder shell fragments fly overhead and then shower and injure charging natives, forcing their retreat.

Clicketty-click! Clicketty-click! Clicketty, clicketty, clicketty-click! The young rim-beating drummers set the pace, racing next to the 3rd Sub-legion.

Captain Kingsbury's yellow-cap, horseback dragoons and running infantry move forward ahead of Wilkinson's slow-arriving 1st Sub-legion and charge in attack mode.

A rider bringing a message from the left tells of flanking attempts in the thick forests by British, Mingo, Mohawk and Wyandotte.

"Hamtramck needs assistance, Lewis!" yells Wayne. "Send the 2nd Sub-legion on the double to the left of the green caps!"

Sounds of bugles communicating orders from Wayne penetrate the hundreds of musket shots being heard.

"General Scott! General Scott!"

"Right here, Anthony."

"Send General Todd's Kentuckians to the left of the red caps. We cannot let the Brits turn our left flank!"

As Scott rides off, General Wayne focuses his attention to what is in front of him a mere 300 yards.

"Bring all your howitzers to the front, Burbeck. We need to support the 4th's movement to the center!"

"General! Move back! You're getting too close! You'll get hit!" warns William Henry Harrison, grabbing Wayne's horse.

"Let go of me! Let go! Dad burnit, Harrison! If such a thing happens, Lieutenant," says Wayne, pulling his reins away, "the standing order is to charge the dang rascals with the bayonet!"

"Our sixteen cannons are at your disposal, General," announces Major Burbeck.

"Fire into the forest and the fallen timbers, Burbeck, straight ahead, same trajectory and to the left ten degrees. Eight cannons each direction. Commence firing until I tell you to stop!"

On the American left that extends two miles north from the Maumee River, the 2nd Sub-legion infantry and dragoons have caught up to support the advance guard of Hamtramck's 4th.

"Farther to the left!" orders General Todd, taking his 550 volunteers to prevent Wyandotte from flanking the American force. "Dismount to get through this forest. If you see red caps, move to their left!" shouts Todd.

Hundreds of high pitched rapid yodel sounds are heard piercing the air.

"We gotta stop, General!" remarks a volunteer. "What is that?"

"Wyandotte. That's their battle cry! Keep moving forward. Keep moving forward, men! Don't be intimidated! Turn their right flank! Sound that bugle, Leroy. Sound the charge!" commands Todd.

"I see redcoats, Gen'ral."

"Good! Let 'em have it, boys!"

BOOM! BOOM! BOOM!

Shell fragments from Burbeck's sixteen artillery pieces shatter limbs above the hunkered-down Miami, Delaware and Shawnee at the center of a mile-and-a-half-long battle line to which they had retreated.

"Tell the green caps to move forward, Harrison!" yells Wayne from behind the artillery. "Cease fire, Burbeck! Send Hamtramck's infantry and dragoons into the fallen trees, Harrison. Root the rascals out! Put them to the bayonet!"

RRum tee-tum tee-tum tee-tum! RRum tee-tum tee-tum tee-tum! RRum tee-tum tee-tum tee-tum!

Young drummers running alongside the dismounted dragoons and infantry into the forest and fallen timber beat the drums that now are dry enough to be heard. The entire bayonet-fixed American line fires off three shots per minute moving forward on the trot, giving the natives no time to effectively reload and return fire.

"Retreat toward the fort!" shouts Shawnee Chiefs Blue Jacket and Black Hoof.

"Ignore them! They are cowards!" yells twenty-six-year-old Tecumseh, holding his ground with tribal kin.

"It is no use, brother. Fall back. There are too many whites!"

"Alright, move back to the next tree. I will cover you!"

Two trees later, Tecumseh does not see his brother Sauwaseekau. Relentless dragoons sprint forward, expelling natives under logs with their musket blades and shooting them in the back as they run zigzagging in retreat.

"Take no captives!" yells a vengeful Uncle Isaac to his fellow dragoons.

"Fight to the finish!" shouts an infantryman.

Pulling up to aim at a reloading Delaware, Uncle Isaac announces, "It's either you or me!" as he squeezes off a round to end the Indian's life.

Through a clearing along the right, 1st and 3rd Sub-legion cavalrymen break through the forest and gallop full stride past the quiet British Fort Miami.

Natives running toward braves gathered around Turkey Foot atop a rock temporarily resist the Americans and then turn to retreat toward Swan Creek.

Breaking out of the forest, Uncle Isaac observes the Fort Miami Union Jack flying and yells, "Let's attack!"

Suddenly, horns blare and drums pound, signaling a halt to the route of the Indians.

"Hold up, men!" orders Captain Kingsbury in sight of the fortress a quarter mile away. "Allow the cavalry to finish up!"

"Ike! Uncle Ike!" calls E.J. with Bobby, sprinting toward the British fort from the ridge line on the right.

"Uncle Isaac! It's me, E.J. How'd you get clear over here?" he says, strolling toward his unmoving, glassy-eyed, speechless uncle.

Hundreds of Americans end the chase and form a colorful white, yellow, green and red semicircle staring at a foreign fort on American soil.

Chapter 15

August 21 – September 14, 1794 — Fort Miami, Fort Defiance and up the Maumee River

Major Price and his scouts, in coordination with Captain Kibbey and his forty, patrol fifteen miles north and west of Fort Miami.

"Don't worry, Wayne knows what he is doing," expresses E.J.

"But why stop us a quarter mile from the fort and then move the legion back into the forest to camp?" asks Bobby. "I didn't see anybody in that fort. We should have walked on in."

"Bobby, you mean you didn't see those cannons sticking out of their bastions? A more urgent question is where have the natives gone?"

"You think they're circling around to attack us from the southwest?"

"Anything's possible, but it's like they disappeared."

"Wow," says Bobby. "That's a big body of water the Maumee flows into!"

"That's Lake Erie, if I remember my geography right," replies E.J.

"Mr. Bevan, tell me what you know about this Fort Miami you deserted from," asks General Wayne atop his steed, examining the fort with his spyglasses.

Not believing he is standing next to the American General, Bevan begins, "I-I-I'm just a musician, but it seems like everyone is sick in there."

"Don't you lure me into false pretenses and tell me how weak it is, dad burnit, or I'll hang you from that oak tree over there before your next breath."

"Oh no, no, no! I'll tell you everything I know. I want to be an American."

"Go on then, and I'll determine if it fits the story of that French trader Lasselle we caught all dressed up like an Indian."

"What do you want to know, your Excellency."

"What do you think I am, a king?" Several aide-de-camps hide their smile at that comment. "How many are in there, and what kind of power do they have?"

"They have 400 total men, four nine-pounders, six six-pounders, two large howitzers, two swivel guns and plenty of ammunition."

"Sounds like you're more than a musician, Bevan. It's a good thing that info matches Lasselle."

That same day, General Charles Scott and his 800 Kentucky volunteer militia are spread about at the forest perimeter, glaring quietly at the British fortress.

Anthony Wayne, in full dress uniform, approaches the fortress alone, riding his black stallion across the openness. Getting within pistol shot range, Wayne mutters to himself, "Why, you low-down dirty redcoats." Turning his horse to walk it around the fort, he mumbles, "You call this a fort, dad burnit?"

Circling the portion that overlooks the Maumee, Wayne examines the water gate for weaknesses and strengths.

Thirty minutes of anxiety from his staff goes by, and the general slowly rides back to his aides-de-camp at the edge of the forest.

"There is a time to be born and a time to die, a time to plant and a time to uproot, a time to kill and a time to heal," reads the pastor from Ecclesiastes in the Bible to Isaac Carlisle.

Staring at his dragoon's campfire located a mile from Fort Miami, Ike sips his cider.

"I've heard you read those words to those who have lost loved ones, Pastor. But I have taken the lives of others in three separate battles."

"The Bible is truth," says the pastor, "and people seek the truth."

"I don't know what came over me. I think it is just that I have seen so much death in the last five years."

"Your actions are understandable, my son."

"I mean, I've seen Injuns tie men to a pole-- that got slowly roasted by an ever-increasing fire." Sobbing, Ike asks, "When does it end, Pastor? All I wanted to be was a farmer with my own land and raise a God-fearing family."

"I have a feeling, similar to the feeling I had at Yorktown, Isaac. It could be over."

The next day inside Fort Miami, frustration builds.

"The Americans are burning the outbuildings, Major Campbell," delivers a British regular message from the bastion.

"You shouldn't have stopped me from shooting Wayne when I had him in my sights, Major," says a Canadian militia officer.

"So you want me to be responsible for a second war with these colonists, do you? Personally, I think they are bypassing us and heading for Detroit."

"There is no telling what Wayne will do," says a veteran British officer.

"Captain Spears, what does the latest message from Wayne read?" inquires Major Campbell.

"He wants to know why we built this fort on American soil and is asking us to evacuate our fortress and surrender."

"Sir, the Americans are removing and burning the crop remains around the perimeter," informs another bastion observer. "There is smoke coming from McKee's Island. The crops there and buildings are on fire!"

"Captain Spears, take a white flag and ride out to inform the brash, pompous lout that we will not vacate this fort until we get orders from King George III of England himself."

At Wayne's marquee tent one mile from Fort Miami, the American generals meet.

"Well, gentlemen, what would the cost be if we attack?" asks Wayne between sips of his whiskey.

"The scuttle among the men is that we will attack, General," expresses Wilkinson.

"That's good," says Wayne. "I want the men primed if we do strike."

"I would estimate 300 to 400 casualties," says Hamtramck after swallowing hard on his cider. "The howitzers we have won't be powerful enough to damage their walls."

"The white oak they used in parts of their bastions is substantial, but I did notice some weaknesses," comments Wayne.

"A siege of any length of time is not reasonable, Anthony. Our food situation, even after stripping the gardens and fields of crops we can use, is not sustainable," offers General Scott, filling his mug to the brim. "The artillery they have is impressive," asserts General Barbee of the Kentuckians.

"At least the Indians know now that the British can't be trusted," points out Wayne.

After pausing, Wayne continues, "Gentlemen, you all know I have permission to start a war with Britain if I see fit," pronounces Wayne. "You also know any siege here would do that."

The Generals and staff stare at Wayne silently.

The next day, the fear is protecting the backside of Anthony Wayne's army from an Indian attack while it retreats back to Fort Defiance.

"Dad burn, that smoke's bad. I couldn't see a redskin if I tried," complains Bobby, straddling his walking horse.

"I did see one run into Fort Deposit as we left," says E.J. "I think he was looking for food."

"That you, E.J.? Bobby?" calls a familiar voice.

"Private Smith?"

"Man, you boys have tough duty. Not only do you have to watch for Injuns, you have to watch their crops and buildings burn, too?"

"Smitty, where have you been?" asks E.J.

"I'm still helping Wilkinson whenever he needs messages sent back to Fort Washington. I saw your Uncle Isaac a bit ago. He said you were back here."

"Well, keep your eyes peeled with us, Smitty. Injuns are out there following us," warns Bobby.

"I sure will. Dad burn, I thought your unk died at Kekionga."

"Nope, it's a miracle," informs E.J. "You both have something in common."

"Sure do. I told him how I survived my leg wound there."

"Did you see Charlotte back at Fort GreeneVille, Smitty?" queries E.J.

"In fact, I did check on her about a week ago when I went through. Oh, she's getting big! She misses you a lot."

"I miss her, too. Our baby is due in a couple months. When you go through GreeneVille again, tell her the army is heading for Kekionga after a stop at Fort Defiance."

"I will do that."

"Smitty, I think the next few weeks will tell if we have peace."

Sectors on the right flank heading back to Fort Defiance discuss the battle.

"General, the 1st Sub-legion lost twenty men," informs Captain Guion. "Wayne put us in the toughest position."

"I received one message from him the entire battle," complains Wilkinson, "and that was to form a double line. It was like he didn't trust anything we would do."

"I don't think he knew what he was doing. He hardly used his drums," expresses Major Cushing.

"I use the term 'battle' loosely. That was more like a skirmish. Fifteen minutes of fighting and forty-five minutes of chasing!" adds Wilkinson.

"We hardly spent any time looking for the legion dead and wounded afterward, scattered about the forests," alleges Guion.

"Don't worry, boys. It is all going into the next letter back east. The last thing that egocentric needs is to be considered a hero."

At the front of the army, General Wayne rides with his staff trailing behind the band.

"That music always sounds better after a victory," remarks Wayne. "Do you think Julius Caesar felt like this following a triumph?"

"Probably did, General," answers Captain Lewis.

"Lieutenant Harrison, ride back and make sure every corn field, garden, tool and weapon the Indians have on either side of the river is being destroyed and any edible food taken."

"Yes sir."

"Captain DeButts, give me a current casualty count from this last offensive."

"That was a nice ceremony you gave before we left Fort Deposit, sir."

"What's the count, Captain?"

"The legion had 113 casualties, twenty-six of whom were killed. General Scott reports twenty killed or wounded Kentuckians."

"I never get used to brave men giving the ultimate for their cause and country," responds Wayne, peering straight ahead. "How many of the enemy did we get?"

"It's hard to tell about the Indians. Best estimate is twice our casualties."

Three more days of the hungry legion traveling through rain and mud brings Fort Defiance into view.

Boom! Boom! Boom!

Echoing up and down the Maumee and Auglaize Rivers, twelve more unloaded howitzer rounds are discharged as a salute to Wayne's returning army.

"I'm glad we were able to be toward the front to hear that," expresses a smiling E.J.

"Kinda," agrees Bobby, "I know they mean well, but it reminds me of what we went through a few days ago."

"I'm just glad we didn't get to hear those British cannons at Fort Miami," comments Uncle Isaac, who was also brought up front.

"They had some big ones, huh?" asks Private Smith, riding alongside.

Crossing a ford to the fort side of the Maumee, William Henry Harrison joins the four.

"You men are probably wondering why you are together at this time."

"Well, it is a nice reunion, Lieutenant," offers Smith, "but yeah, what's in store for us?"

"You four have been to Kekionga before, were you not?" asks Harrison.

"Yes sir, we were there during General Harmar's campaign," answers Uncle Isaac.

"Since you know those parts, the general would like your knowledge at the front going forward."

"What does that mean, Lieutenant?" voices E.J. with some concern.

"It means you better write your loved ones, 'cause you won't be going back to GreeneVille anytime soon. All four of you have been assigned to the advance guard of Hamtramck's 4th Sub-legion to advise the general's staff as well as Kibbey and Major Price."

"Lieutenant, we don't know much about the route between Fort Defiance and Kekionga."

"Don't worry, not many of us do, but we have some captured Indians that better lead us accurately."

Riding up to the main gate of Fort Defiance, Wayne is not happy.

"What are these wounded and sick men doing out here scattered about? I sent them ahead of the legion a day ago to get some treatment!"

"These men are getting treated. It is just that it's crowded inside the fort."

"We need to get some changes made outside as well as inside," demands Wayne. "Do you see the issue with the walls, Major Burbeck? How are they going to withstand British twelve-pounders?"

"They won't, General. I've been thinking about that during our return. We need a ditch dug around the perimeter and the dirt thrown up against the picket wall for strength. I calculate eight feet deep and twelve feet wide, sir."

"How about building a drawbridge main gate across that ditch?"

"You got it, General, and I suggest adding more howitzers to each blockhouse."

"Yes, we can spare four more. We'll save the rest for the new fort at Kekionga."

"Congratulations, General!" calls William Wells, striding out the main gate with his arm in a sling.

"Wells! Get over here!" yells Wayne, smiling while dismissing Major Burbeck. "You and McClellan ready to go scouting?"

"That would be nice, General, but my arm is useless, and Blue Bird's shoulder is still bad."

"Blue Bird?"

"You'll have to ask him about that. Ha!" responds Wells. "Looks like you got into a tussle up there at Roche de Bout?"

"We had to go a little farther than that. All the injured are going to stay here while the legion and volunteers head to the Miami Towns."

"Take some of these sutlers with you. The money-gouging no-gooders are charging a fortune knowing we're practically on half rations."

"We may take them and give them a gun, Wells. The desertion rate is unacceptable—with some actually heading to join the British!" remarks Wayne disgustedly.

"We have Major Price's scouts leading General Todd's Kentuckians with packhorses back to Fort Adams and Recovery to bring supplies forward."

Two weeks later, in Philadelphia, word is received.

"Mr. President, the Indians have been routed along a place the natives call the Standing Rock River, near Lake Erie. I just got the news," says Secretary of War Henry Knox, handing the letter to Washington.

"Let me see that."

"The British stayed in their fort. They offered very little help to the natives. Wayne is very proud of the men, their performance was gallant."

"This is a far cry from the letters we have received from General Wilkinson. I was beginning to think Wayne might have been a wrong choice and a second war with England was imminent."

"I suggest we send a letter authorizing him to negotiate a treaty among those native aggressors," voices Knox.

"Yes, get it off today. But I still want that fort built at the Miami Towns. That will send a strong message to the natives as well as the British that that's American land."

Back at Fort Defiance, what is left of Wayne's 2500-man mix of legionnaires and volunteers prepares to depart.

"Major Price, I want you to escort this squaw that Wells brought us a few weeks ago. Take her partway to the Roche de Bout with this letter I've written offering peace. Here is another one she can deliver to our captured Frenchman Antoine Lasselle's brother."

"I thought you hung him, General."

"Nah, probably should have. He'll make a good trade. Be careful, Major, there are still renegade Injuns not happy about the results at the fallen timbers."

Price salutes and gallops away with the squaw.

"Hey, Major Burbeck, I like the improvements you've made in the fort."

"Thank you, sir."

"General Scott, I appreciate your General Todd bringing sheep, cattle and the packhorses forward, but according to quartermaster O'Hara, that delivery will only last us two weeks."

"Yes, Anthony. We're going to need more," answers Scott.

"Send General Barbee and his command this time to bring more packhorses with supplies, and have the men carry flour bags on their mount. They will be paid extra for that."

"How about some whiskey, too?" asks Scott. "These restless volunteers may be more manageable."

"Did you hear that, O'Hara?" yells Wayne. "We need some more packhorses and whiskey, dad burnit!"

"Yes sir. I'll do my best. Somehow orders going to Fort Washington are getting mixed up," asserts Colonel O'Hara, glancing at personnel finishing final preparations to head for Kekionga.

"Contractors Elliott and Williams ought to be fired!" pronounces Wayne. "Alright, Barbee, get heading south through the swamp, but return on Harmar's trail and meet us with fresh supplies at Kekionga."

"Yes sir."

"Major Hunt, we're about to leave. If any Indian chiefs show up to negotiate, tell them where the legion went. If the British show up, tell them to kiss my rear end!"

Chapter 16

September 15 – October 22, 1794 — Along the Maumee River and the Kekionga area (Present-day Fort Wayne, Indiana)

Six war-painted Miami Indians follow the legion from Fort Defiance toward Kekionga.

"Grey Wolf, do you see their scout?"

"Yes, I see him, Running Deer. Rarely does one see the Americans without another nearby."

"Occasionally, there is a gap. We could slip inside their perimeter and take out Wayne."

"I know how much you despise the whites on our land, but there are only six of us warriors, eight total, including Morning Bird and my wife."

"Hundreds of brothers who ran from the battlefield at the fallen timbers, in my mind, did so to fight another day," responds Running Deer.

"My friend, the coalition has scattered. They've gone home. Their vengeance was taken out on the seven whites burned at the stake at Lake Erie recently," states the Algonquin-speaking Grey Wolf.

"If we can eliminate the black snake, that would be incentive for the confederation of Indians and British to reunite."

"That will be difficult, Running Deer. Some of our people shot our own at Fort Recovery."

"I know. I still regret not ending the life of the big Chippewa when I had the chance."

The twisting Maumee River forces the trailblazing pioneers to cut tangents through the forests between river bends.

"We're going to have to fire off a gunshot occasionally so the 1st and 4th on the wings know where the main column is," orders General Wayne.

"General, some of these ravines we're taking are hard on the wagons and horses. Any thoughts on crossing over to the south side of the river and following that trail?" asks aid- de-camp DeButts.

"Scouts say it is swampier over there, and dad burn," says Wayne scanning the forest canopy, "we've already had enough of these tree snakes falling on us. Use the 3rd Sub-legion to push the wagons from behind when necessary.

"Get that band to play a little louder, Captain! Perhaps it will take the men's minds off the difficulties."

Late on the third day of Wayne's trek from Fort Defiance, familiar landmarks appear.

"Sergeant Carlisle, Kibbey's scouts tell me you are correct. The confluence of the river is a couple miles ahead," affirms Lieutenant Harrison.

"Not only that, Lieutenant," offers Uncle Isaac, "we're beginning to pass through the old Shawnee town they called Chillicothe."

"Yes," adds Bobby. "There was a small village of Delaware living on the other side of the river, too."

"It's overgrown around here now, Lieutenant," pronounces Private Smith. "It was similar in size to Kekionga. Harmar's army wreaked havoc on this place. I have to admit, I helped torch it."

"If you've seen the sketch Lieutenant Denny made of the Miami towns four years ago, you'll know where the gardens and cornfields of the upcoming Kekionga village were," offers E.J.

Following the trail next to the Maumee on the left, silence from being tired after a long day dominates the advance guard. Behind, the band faintly heard leading the legion now features the drummers, who are maintaining the pace.

Breaking the conversational silence, E.J. comments, "Hopefully, the scouts have located what we called Harmar's ford up ahead. We can cross there to the south side and up the riverbank."

"Okay, It's getting dark, and General Wayne has expressed he does not wish to camp in the battlefield. He wants the high ground for defensive purposes."

"It will be sand dune-like, Lieutenant, but it is forested with Indian trails going everywhere," relates Uncle Isaac.

"Thanks, Mr. Carlisle. That's good information. I'm sure the general would like to pitch the tents tonight and examine Kekionga tomorrow."

Early the next morning, a half mile downstream from the confluence of the St. Joseph and St. Marys Rivers, Native Indians hidden in dense forest watch Americans wading in the river.

"What are they doing this early?" asks Grey Wolf.

"That is where the attack of Harmar's army began," informs Running Deer.

"Are they going to build a bridge or dam there?"

"Maybe someday," responds Running Deer, "but I would say they are collecting the remains of the whites we killed when Harmar's army crossed to butcher our people in Kekionga."

"I am glad our Kitchi Manitou does not allow us to touch the evil whites' bones and skulls," conveys Grey Wolf.

"There are more dead Americans in the river up the St. Joseph about a mile, where the battle ended."

"In fact, dead Americans are spread throughout Kekionga," adds Morning Bird, waking up and overhearing the conversation.

"Who is that crouched and walking in the thorn crabs and plum trees on the other side of the river? Do you see him heading slowly toward the Americans?" asks Grey Wolf. "Is he one of ours?"

"Yes," answers Running Deer, glancing back at his camp. "We have a brother missing."

"Here are some," says Bobby, collecting femur and humerus bones and placing them in an empty flour bag.

"I wish we had something better to carry them with," says the pastor.

"It's respectful to take care of these remains before the camp wakes up," comments E.J.

"Perhaps it would be better for the army to see these. So they know the commitment the previous soldiers had," remarks Uncle Isaac.

"Ike, if you don't want to go with us up the St. Joseph to find Ben, we'll understand," says Bobby.

"This is tougher than I thought, boys. All these bones and skulls busted up. Same thing could have happened to me if I had been discovered pinned under my horse."

"My concern," laments the pastor, "is that some of these men who died here may not have accepted Jesus as their lord and savior."

BAM! A shot echoes from downstream.

Uncle Isaac surveys the banks while instinctively raising his rifle.

"Crap, where did that come from?" wonders E.J. aloud, peering around and cocking his musket, then noticing gun smoke in the distance.

With a splash, the pastor falls facedown into the shallow river.

"Pastor!" calls Bobby. "Pastor!"

"Hold my gun, E.J.," requests Uncle Isaac. Rolling the pastor over, Ike holds him up out of the water. The trio notice red oozing from his chest.

Later that morning in Anthony Wayne's marquee, a gout-inflicted general holds a meeting.

"The pastor was a good man. Weren't the scouts out this morning? Didn't we have men on guard duty?" asks Wayne, hobbling while hanging onto his portable bed frame.

"The area had been scouted yesterday late afternoon. A few French trappers and a rogue Indian or two were noticed, but no large party of warriors had been seen, sir," answers Thomas Lewis.

"Captain, everyone was tired yesterday after seventeen miles, but dad burnit, the one time we don't set up defensive breastworks around our camp, somebody gets killed."

"We are still at war, men," renders Harrison. "We cannot let our guard down."

"You're right, Harrison. Kibbey, Price and the Kentuckians are out scouring the Miami towns looking for the assassin as we speak. The next one shot could be any one of us.

"Major Burbeck," continues Wayne, "as soon as we get saddled, we will begin selecting a suitable fort site. Meanwhile, think about a regular fortress that is able to withstand British bombardment. Place a bastion at each corner, and I want a blockhouse separate from the fort near the closest point of the Maumee.

Two days later, General Barbee and supplies on packhorses arrive, along with mounted Kentucky militia.

"Dad burn, if you aren't a welcome site," greets General Charles Scott. "See the larger tent?" directs Scott. "The flour goes there, and the cattle you bring give us forty-four beeves. They are pasturing on the south side of camp."

"Where's Wayne?" asks Barbee.

"He's out with Major Burbeck marking trees to be cut for the fort," answers Captain DeButts.

"He won't be happy about the sutlers that followed us in. Seventy-five cents for a pound of bacon, and whiskey, for crying out loud, is eight dollars a gallon!"

"Soldiers won't be happy either," responds Scott, "nobody has that kind of money!"

"We'll have to stay on half rations. Your supply is still not enough to sustain 2500 men for very long," asserts DeButts. "We've been making some calculations. Wayne wants to send back General Todd and Price with their companies for more supplies tomorrow morning. This time they'll go to GreeneVille."

Two days later, a mile up the St. Joseph, water is shallow enough to search.

"Smitty, you didn't get up this far during the battle, did you?" asks E.J., wading and gathering bones.

"Naw, I went down at the beginning at Harmar's ford. Laid along that river till nightfall. You can't believe what I saw."

"Yes, I can. I saw Ben … well, you know."

"We all have seen more than we need to in the last few years," adds Bobby.

"We've collected quite a bit here. Let's check up on the bank where Ike's charge took place," imparts E.J. "Unless the Injuns busted up Ben, I might be able to recognize his skull."

"The pastor would appreciate all the soldiers we've gathered being buried next to him," expresses Bobby.

"I agree. It's going to take a while to get over him being gone. But at least we can put some closure on things."

During the next six days, the forests surrounding the cleared fort site contain all available men to cut and haul logs.

"This would be the time to be on guard duty, Bobby," says E.J.

"I'm glad they captured some warriors that may have been the shooter, but you're right, E.J., this is no picnic."

"Horses are dyin' off, boys. Been overworked," says Private Smith.

"Let's trim this one up and cut down one more, and then let's take a break," suggests E.J.

"Dad-burned militias are ready to head home," comments Smith. "The enlistment time is about to expire for legion folks, too. They're all getting homesick."

"We better get new recruits in, or the British will have an easy time of it if they decide to come up river," advises Bobby.

"Geez, I wonder how Charlotte is?" utters E.J., chopping off the last branch of a log destined for the fort parapet.

"Well, at least we are near the fort site and don't have to carry it far," remarks Bobby.

"Alright, let's bring this big oak down," says E.J. while throwing his ax into the side of the trunk.

Bobby axes the other side, and soon the tree begins to wobble.

"Arrete! No more, stop! Ici!" expresses a voice from the top of the tree.

"You hear somethin'?" asks Smitty.

"It's from up there, someone's up there," informs Bobby.

Stepping back, E.J. yells, "Get down here!"

"No, no!" calls the voice back.

"Okay!" E.J. responds and begins chopping again.

"Ici! Stop! Vers le bas!"

"There he comes," states Bobby. "It's an Indian."

"Sounded like he was speaking French," comments Smitty.

Guard duty personnel show up after noticing the commotion and work stoppage. The Miami brave is taken to the blockhouse being used as the guardhouse and is tied up.

A week goes by at Kekionga, and the new fort has progressed enough for a detachment of generals and officers to follow the portage from the St. Marys River to the Little Wabash River.

"Lead the way, Captain Kibbey. Take us to the put-in place," orders General Wayne, crossing a St. Marys ford by horseback.

Riding up the riverbank and reaching the top, numerous campsites and a trail heading southwest are spotted.

"As you will see, the passage is well worn," comments Kibbey. "I 'm taking men to scout ahead, General. Water will be shallow this time of year. Just stay on the higher-ground path. It will be about eight miles in length."

"Word is, General," speaks Lieutenant Harrison, "the Miami have controlled this passage for about a hundred years, and currently, Chief Richardville and his mother, Tah Cum Wah, who is a sister of Little Turtle, charge users of the portage a fee. They also offer the services of Miami Indians to carry trade goods and boats in each direction."

"Sounds like a lucrative business," comments Wayne. "I'd like to meet them two."

While the detachment of Americans ride three abreast, Wayne continues his thoughts. "Harrison, when we get back to Kekionga, what are your views on having a bateau built to transport supplies on the Maumee to Fort Defiance from Kekionga."

"General, not much doubt in my mind, when the water is higher, we could even transport supplies by boat up the Miami River from Cincinnati, then portage to the St. Marys and float to Kekionga," expresses Harrison.

As the U.S contingent of officers travel the path thick forests are noted and then marshy wetlands indicating a watershed that goes either to the Wabash or the St.Marys.

"Hold up," orders Wayne. "Here's Kibbey. End of the line, Captain?"

"Here's one of a couple places they put in, General."

"Make note, DeButts, that a blockhouse might be a good thing to have at this end."

The men detect a vacant camp and trails striking off in different directions.

"Alright, I've seen enough. Let's head back. Dad burnit, they better be making some progress on that fort."

Two days later, during the commotion of the militia returning from GreeneVille with packhorses and wagons loaded with supplies and new settlers, E.J. makes a visit to the guardhouse near the river.

"Why are you tied out here?" asks E.J.

"Whites on the inside don't like me. How do you know I speak English?" responds the Indian.

"You were yelling some of it from the top of that oak tree, ya fool," says a half-smiling E.J., offering some beef jerky.

"Also some French," tells the Indian, taking a bite. "I wanted to make sure you understood me."

"Your painted face looks familiar. Who are you, and where are you from?"

"My people call me Running Deer. I am Miami, and I grew up in Kekionga."

"I fought you in the battle here, didn't I? That's where I've seen you before."

"E.J.! E.J.!" interrupts a voice, dashing toward him down a sandy riverbank.

"What's going on, Bobby?"

"You won't believe who showed up and what just happened."

Nodding goodbye to Running Deer and turning to join Bobby, E.J. walks up the bank listening.

"Come on, Buddy!"

"Well, tell me," demands E.J.

"Charlotte and Phillip just showed up in one of the supply wagons!"

"What? Where they at?"

"Come on, follow me. And guess what?"

"Not again. What?"

"You're a father!"

At the fort being constructed overlooking the three rivers, Wayne and Burbeck conduct business.

"That ditch around the fort needs to be deeper, Burbeck, dag nabbit! I want it fourteen feet wide, also. Have them throw the dirt between the two picket walls for reinforcement."

"Dad burn, General, you'd think this is my first fort!"

"I know, I know," responds Wayne. "It's my gout and the dad-burned militia around here raising cane. Last night, somebody hung the horns of a stolen bull they ate above my tent entryway. The culprits will be hung when they are caught. I know people are hungry, but we can't have cattle rustling."

"You men!" yells Burbeck. "Be careful rolling those howitzers up onto the bastion. Get some help, dad burnit! Get those guys carrying ammunition to help you push it up the ramp!

"Might as well send the militia home, General. Their time is up," suggests Major Burbeck.

"They will be in two days. Major Price is leading Scott and the Kentuckians back to Fort Washington for dismissal. That'll make about a thousand less men around here to feed."

"In a few days, this fort will be done. You sticking around, General, waiting for word from the Indians about signing a treaty?"

"No Major, I'm going to leave 300 troops here under Colonel Hamtramck and take the rest of the legion back to GreeneVille. That will be closer to supplies and Cincinnati. Injuns can find us there."

"Hello, Phillip!" greets a hurrying E.J. with Bobby trotting behind him. Hugging his now nine-year-old brother-in-law standing outside a covered wagon, E.J. hears a baby's cry from inside.

"Charlotte, can I come in?" asks E.J.

"She's nodding yes," says a midwife inside as a doctor climbs off the wagon, smiling.

"You got a name picked out for that little boy?" asks the doctor.

"I need to see Charlotte first," explains E.J., stepping into the back of the Conestoga.

After hugging and kissing, Charlotte hands the swaddled baby to E.J.

"What do you think?" asks Charlotte.

"He looks fine and healthy," says a grinning E.J.

"No, about a name."

"Hmm, I'd say Wayne Pastor Carlisle."

A week later, early in the morning of October 22, an assembly of more than 1000 soldiers and citizenry stand outside the newly built fort gates.

"Charlotte, you find a good spot to hear these proceedings, and I'll be back," says E.J., handing the baby to his wife standing next to Phillip.

"Okay, E.J. You stand tall. I'm very proud of you!" she calls as E.J. sprints away.

"It is more than appropriate that we dedicate this fort on these very grounds on the very day that, in 1790, General Josiah Harmar's army was engaged with the enemy here at Kekionga!" proclaims Lieutenant Colonel John Hamtramck.

While the ceremony takes place, E.J. jogs down the bank toward the guardhouse to Running Deer tied to a pole with his hands behind his back.

Drawing his scalping knife, E.J. approaches the Indian.

"What do you want, white man," asks the Miami, "to end my sadness by taking my life?"

From a distance Hamtramck's voice carries.

"I now commission this fort and name it after the general who marched us to victory through the wilderness. I declare this garrison Fort Wayne!"

BOOM! BOOM!

"No, Running Deer, I'm going to cut you loose."

"You are?"

BOOM! BOOM! BOOM! Around the four bastions of Fort Wayne, the howitzers fire.

E.J. stops cutting halfway through the leather to look in Running Deer's face and make a request.

"You must promise me that you will strive for peace with your people."

Chapter 17

Late winter 1915 — East central district, Fort Wayne, Indiana

A large gathering takes place inside Mrs. Harrington's home.

"My husband would never do anything like that! Oh dear," she says.

"You sure you never heard any screaming or yelling down in the cellar, Mrs. Harrington?"

"Take it easy, Deputy Sheriff Bork," requests Fort Wayne Chief of Police John Wynn. "Besides, you're inside city limits, and I can take it from here."

"The only thing my dear husband and his friends would yell about would be a winning poker hand."

"Gambling, huh?" asks the deputy.

"Whatever happened to Sheriff Reichelderfer?" asks Nyle. "He would be humoring us about finding pioneer remains around this town."

"Reichelderfer? Sheriff Gladieux beat him out in the last election. He didn't take this job seriously enough!" expresses the high-strung Bork. "Gambling—gambling, my son—is against the law and is no humorous matter."

"Dad burnit, Deputy, will you lighten up? Can't you see Mrs. Harrington is in mourning, and this isn't helping anything?" remarks Wynn.

"Police Chief Wynn, you have about fifteen human skulls in the basement, and you want me to lighten up?"

"Oh dear, fifteen? You boys didn't tell me there is that many. Oh, I'm feeling a bit faint."

"Now, now, Mrs. Harrington, it will be okay," assures Bob Gavin, the local amateur historian.

"Yeah, Mrs. Harrington. All these skulls have gashes and cracks in them from old war battles," says Nyle's brother Stan, "and we didn't find any scalping knives down in the basement, unless your husband hid them."

Mrs. Harrington faints and falls behind into her rocking chair, almost tipping over backwards.

"Now look what you boys have done!" declares Chief Wynn, grabbing the rocker and fanning the lady with his cap.

"I told you, he was a collector of old... let's just say artifacts, just like a lot of guys around this town," conveys Mr. Gavin.

"To be sure, we could bring in a forensic anthropologist-type person to examine these skulls and then find them a nice burial spot," suggests the police chief.

"I'd like to know where the rest of the skeletal remains are," remarks the deputy.

Two weeks later, after historians and experts have visited Mrs. Harrington's basement to make their examinations and assessments, the undertakers arrive.

"I could've told those so-called officials these skulls are old," says Josh to his partner, preparing a stretcher on which to place the skulls.

"We've removed a lot of this type of thing from many a digging site, and the remains all look alike to me," asserts co-worker Jake. "Too bad we have to always do this at night to avoid the curious."

"That poor Mrs. Harrington, above us walking around, having to endure all the commotion these last few days," renders Josh, placing a skull on the stretcher.

"What about living above these skulls for who knows how many years?"

"A lot of people, all over this town, don't realize what could be buried underneath them."

The light bulb in the basement flickers and goes out.

"Dang, you got a flashlight, Jake?" asks Josh nervously.

"Yes, but it's an old one. Here, you take it, and I'll get our lantern from the truck so we don't bother Mrs. Harrington. I think she's gone to bed."

Leaving and returning by the outside cellar door, Jake hangs the lantern, casting eerie shadows.

"Let's finish this up, Josh. I don't feel comfortable down here, and the street lighting outside isn't working either," informs Jake.

"*You* don't feel comfortable? I had to stay down here while you went for the lantern."

"As much as we've done this kind of work, you'd think we'd get used to it," reasons Jake.

"Remember those voices we heard at that one site a couple years ago?" asks Josh.

"Don't remind me."

"Okay, let's see if we can't carry all these skulls out of here in one trip?" suggests Josh.

"Alright, pick the stretcher up on three," orders Jake.

"One, two, three," they say together and move toward the exit carefully just as Bob Gavin walks in carrying a flashlight.

"You guys down here?!"

Startled, the undertakers jerk and stagger, spilling the skulls.

"Dang, sorry men," says Gavin, observing the scattered skulls. "I told Mrs. Harrington I'd stop and check on things."

"Ahhh, that's okay mister, b-but," stammers Jake, "did you see that skull with the bashed temple smile?"

"I ... I was gonna ask you the same thing."

Accreditation and Further Reading

Baldwin, Leland D. *The Keelboat Age on Western Waters.* Pittsburgh, PA: University of Pittsburgh Press, 1941.

Brice, Wallace. *History of Fort Wayne.* Fort Wayne, IN: D.W. Jones and Son, Steam Book and Job Printers, 1868.

Downes, Robert. *"The Indians in Winter."* http://northernexpress.com. March 13, 2011.

Feng, Patrick. *"The Battle of the Wabash."* http://armyhistory.org. July 16, 2014.

Font, Walter, ed. *A Garrison at Miami Town.* Fort Wayne, IN: Allen County-Fort Wayne Historical Society, 1994.

Gaff, Alan. *Bayonets in the Wilderness: Anthony Wayne's Legion in the Old West.* Norman, OK: University of Oklahoma Press, 2004.

Gale, Neil. *"William Wells taken Captive by Miami and Delaware Indians at Thirteen Years. Indian Warrior, fights for U.S. at the Fort Dearborn Massacre with a Detailed Account."* http://drloihjournal.blogspot.com. *July 10, 2018.*

Griswold, Bert J. *The Pictorial History of Fort Wayne, Indiana.* Chicago, IL: Robert O. Law, 1917.

Hogeland, William. *Autumn of the Black Snake.* New York, NY: Farrar, Straus and Giroux, 2017.

Linklatter, Andro. *"The Man Who Double crossed the Founders; An Artist in Treason: The Extraordinary Double Life of General James Wilkinson."* NPR Radio. http://npr.org. April 28, 2010.

McGrane, R.C. *William Clark's Journal of General Wayne's Campaign.* Oxford, England: Oxford University Press, 1914.

National Science Foundation. *"The Lenape Talking Dictionary."* http://talk-lenape.org. 2019

Platt, Carolyn V. *"The Great Black Swamp."* http://newbremenhistory.org. February-March, 1987.

Poinsatte, Charles. *Outpost in the Wilderness: Fort Wayne 1706-1828.* Fort Wayne, IN: Allen County, Fort Wayne Historical Society, 1976.

Seelinger, Matthew. *"The Battle of Fallen Timbers, 20 August 1794."* http://armyhistory.org. July 16, 2014.

Sword, Wiley. *President Washington's Indian War: The Struggle for the Old Northwest, 1790-1795.* Norman, OK: University of Oklahoma Press, 1985.

Tanner, Helen Hornbeck, ed. *Atlas of Great Lakes Indian History.* Norman, OK: University of Oklahoma Press, 1987.

The Holy Bible

Wilson, Frazier E. *Journal of Captain Daniel Bradley, An Epic of the Ohio Frontier.* GreeneVille, OH: F.H. Jobes and Sons, 1935.

Young, Calvin M. *Little Turtle: The Great Chief of the Miami Indian Nation.* GreeneVille, OH: Calvin M. Young, 1917.